# CHERRY AMES, BOARDING SCHOOL NURSE

## *The* Cherry Ames *Stories*

Cherry Ames, Student Nurse
Cherry Ames, Senior Nurse
Cherry Ames, Army Nurse
Cherry Ames, Chief Nurse
Cherry Ames, Flight Nurse
Cherry Ames, Veterans' Nurse
Cherry Ames, Private Duty Nurse
Cherry Ames, Visiting Nurse
Cherry Ames, Cruise Nurse
Cherry Ames at Spencer
Cherry Ames, Night Supervisor
Cherry Ames, Mountaineer Nurse
Cherry Ames, Clinic Nurse
Cherry Ames, Dude Ranch Nurse
Cherry Ames, Rest Home Nurse
Cherry Ames, Country Doctor's Nurse
Cherry Ames, Boarding School Nurse

☆ ☆ ☆

## *The* Vicki Barr *Flight Stewardess Series*

Silver Wings for Vicki
Vicki Finds the Answer
The Hidden Valley Mystery
The Secret of Magnolia Manor
The Clue of the Broken Blossom
Behind the White Veil
The Mystery at Hartwood House
Peril Over the Airport
The Mystery of the Vanishing Lady
The Search for the Missing Twin

*"The book says, 'Store in a cool, dark place.'"*

# CHERRY AMES BOARDING SCHOOL NURSE

*By*

HELEN WELLS

NEW YORK

GROSSET & DUNLAP

*Publishers*

PRINTED IN THE UNITED STATES OF AMERICA

# Contents

# CHERRY AMES, BOARDING SCHOOL NURSE

CHAPTER I

# Lisette

CHERRY WISHED THE TRAIN WOULD GO FASTER. SHE was still out of breath from running for it. She pressed her cheek against the window to admire the green fields and fertile farms through which the local train poked along. Cherry's mother, who knew the headmistress of the Jamestown School for Girls from their own school days, had warned her that the school was deep in the country. Fortunately, it was not too far from Hilton, Illinois, which meant that she would be able to spend all school holiday vacations at home.

As the boarding school nurse, she would have full charge of the school infirmary. It would be fun to work with young people and a refreshing change from her last job—an unexpectedly thrilling assignment as nurse to a country doctor—something new, something different. If there was anything Cherry enjoyed, it was meeting new people. She was glad that she was a nurse because nursing, in its many branches, provided an *Open sesame* to new and exciting experiences—and because more importantly, a nurse can help to alleviate human suffering. She remembered what her twin brother Charlie had said jokingly when he put her on this train in Hilton:

"Don't set this boarding school on its ear. Wherever you go, twin, you make things happen, but you bring doggoned good nursing too."

It gave Cherry a good, warm feeling to know that her pilot brother, and her parents, too, were proud of her. They had made that clear during this past week, when they'd had such a satisfying family reunion, in their big, old-fashioned house. The week's rest had left Cherry's cheeks glowing rose-red and her black eyes sparkling. Even her jet-black curls shone with extra good health. She felt fully ready to tackle her new job.

She stood up, slim and tall, to stretch for a moment and noticed again the girl at the other end of the car. Only about fourteen years old, and small for her age, she was absorbed in a thick volume which lay open on her knees. The girl leafed through several pages, then as if finding what she sought, read eagerly—leafed, read, searched again. She read, Cherry thought idly, as if that book held all the answers to all her questions—whatever they were.

When the train pulled into Jamestown, Cherry noticed that the girl was getting off, too. They were the only two passengers who alighted. Jamestown consisted of a crossroads and a few stores, sheltered by magnificent oak trees. Only a few farmers, driving in for supplies, were outdoors in the heat of the afternoon. Cherry looked around for a station wagon or other car from the school, half expecting to be met. Hadn't Mrs. Harrison received her telegram? Perhaps she should telephone the school. Then Cherry spied a sedan with a sign in its windshield: *Taxi.*

But the young girl from the train was already making arrangements with the taxi driver. Cherry heard her say:

"—to the school, the Jamestown School."

Cherry approached them uncertainly. This was probably the one and only taxi in town, and in the country people often shared rides.

"I beg your pardon, but I'm going to the school, too, and since there's no school car here, I wonder—"

"Please share the taxi with me," the girl said at once and pleasantly.

So they stepped in and settled back. The driver started off through leafy tunnels formed by the arching oaks. Cherry and the young girl did not speak for several minutes. It was one of those ripe, golden afternoons when it feels as if summer will last forever, yet the school term would begin within a few days. Cherry was arriving early in order to get the infirmary in good shape, but what was a student doing here so early, she wondered.

Cherry glanced at the girl who had drawn away into her own corner of the seat. She was slight and pale, with a cloud of dark hair falling onto her shoulders.

"Since we're both going to the school," Cherry offered, "we might introduce ourselves. I'm Cherry Ames."

The girl smiled. "I'm Lisette Gauthier." She was rather shy. "Is this your first time at the school?"

"Yes, it is. Yours, too?"

"Yes, Miss Ames." The girl glanced away, hugging the big book to her. She seemed to be struggling with shyness, then overcame it in a rush. "I came to the school a week early, you know." She did not say why. "I went into Riverton to do some errands, and to visit the library. It's bigger than the school library."

"What an eager student!" Cherry exclaimed. "Studying before the term even begins."

"Oh—no—I mean, yes. It isn't exactly studying." Lisette did not reveal what the thick book was. After that, the girl sat quiet and guarded in her corner.

The taxi drove on past gardens where the scent of flowers floated on the air. Cherry remarked on the delicious fragrance, and—to choose another safe conversational subject—she mentioned her contact with Mrs. Harrison, the headmistress and owner of the Jamestown School.

"I've never met Mrs. Harrison but her letters have been awfully nice," Cherry said. "I'm looking forward to meeting her this afternoon."

Lisette turned and this time her smile had real warmth. "Everyone loves Mrs. Harrison. You will, too, I know you will. She's—well, you'll see! Can you imagine anyone else who'd let me come to the chateau a week early, and who'd even—"

The girl broke off, as if she had been about to say too much. Cherry filled the embarrassed silence with a cheerful remark about the fun of starting a new term, especially at a new school. Lisette looked at her with gratitude. Her eyes were ebony black and seemed to fill her ivory face. A funny little sprite, Cherry thought, first too shy to talk, then talking *almost* too much . . .

All of a sudden the taxi slowed, and the driver, grumbling, coasted the car to the side of the road and hopped out for a look at the motor. He poked and examined and then went to peer in the gas tank.

"But the gas gauge reads better'n half full," he muttered.

Cherry glanced at it. So it did.

"Gauge isn't workin'," the driver said. "Gas tank is bone dry. I'll have to go for gas. A mile's walk in this broiling sun to the nearest gas station!"

He stamped off, carrying a metal container. The two girls were left alone together in the back seat of the sedan. Trees shaded them, but still it was going to be a long, warm wait.

"What wouldn't I give for a soda right now!" Cherry said. "Chocolate for you?"

"Chocolate for me," Lisette agreed. Her eyes danced

like Cherry's own. She glanced at Cherry with obvious curiosity, although it was apparent that she would never intrude with questions. Cherry tried to ease things for her.

"You think I'm one of the new teachers, don't you?"

"Well, you look a little bit too young and too—"

"Too what?" Cherry laughed.

Lisette swallowed. "Too young and gay."

"To tell you the truth, I'm to be the school nurse."

"Oh! That's nice. I've always sort of wanted to be a nurse."

"Lots of girls want to," Cherry replied. "A lot of them really do it, too."

"It's a sympathetic profession," Lisette said thoughtfully. "I always think of a nurse as a friend."

"Well, I hope you and I will be friends."

Lisette responded with such a glowing face that Cherry could not help but respond, too.

"I don't think," Lisette said very seriously, "that a few years' difference in our ages is important." She pretended to be busy adjusting the car window. "Do you?"

"Of course not."

Then Lisette was telling her, as fast as the words would tumble out, about her scholarship and her family and her wonderful luck in coming to the Jamestown School.

"All my life I've wanted to come here! And father always wanted me to attend boarding school. A really good one! I couldn't tell this to everybody, Miss Ames, but honestly, I'd never be here if it had been left up to my poor papa." She said *papa,* French fashion. "It's the greatest luck that I've a scholarship. Imagine. A year's scholarship and my room in the dormitory, everything, a regular guest!"

"It *is* wonderful," Cherry said. "I didn't know boarding schools gave scholarships."

"They don't very often. It's just that Mrs. Harrison is so generous. Not that she can afford—I mean—"

Lisette broke off short again.

Cherry's curiosity was aroused. How did the girl know what Mrs. Harrison could afford if she was a newcomer to the school? Then, too, what was she doing here a week early? Was it because of some family problem?

"What about your *papa?*" Cherry asked, since it was obvious that Lisette was trying to change the subject. "What a cunning way to say it!"

"We spoke French a good deal at home in St. Louis," Lisette said. "Especially Papa. He spoke beautiful French, although he was American-born. And he was a delightful host, and he knew dozens of funny stories, but that's about all Papa could do. He just wasn't a practical man. He tried hard to earn a living, but— My heavens, I *am* telling you a lot, Miss Ames."

"I'll respect your confidence." Cherry thought the girl must be starved for companionship, she seemed to be so glad to make a new friend. "By the way, wouldn't you rather call me Miss Cherry? It's friendlier."

Lisette looked pleased but suddenly shy again.

"You say your father *was* and *had*," Cherry prompted.

"He died three years ago," Lisette told her.

"Forgive me. You must miss him very much."

"Yes, we do. It's hardest on Mother. For another reason, too. She's had to earn our living, you see—Papa only left us a tiny bit of insurance. And a collection of beautiful books of poetry," Lisette said wryly. "Mother says one can't be angry with a dreamer who simply couldn't cope with life. Papa did mean well." Lisette's voice trailed off.

"Is your mother in business?" Cherry asked.

"She gives music lessons."

No wonder Lisette was in need of a scholarship, Cherry thought. Teaching music was, as a rule, an uncertain way to make a small living.

Lisette was saying much the same thing, but in words chosen to save her pride. Her mother had made all of Lisette's dresses for the coming school year—it was less expensive than buying the dresses at a shop. Lisette hoped that her mother would come to visit her at the school, but she was busy with her pupils, and then there was the matter of fare. It was clear to Cherry that Mrs. Gauthier was making a sacrifice to send Lisette away to boarding school, even with the aid of a scholarship.

"I'm going to make this year count," Lisette told Cherry earnestly. "It's my big chance. I *must* make it count."

"I'm sure that you will," Cherry encouraged her. "Attending a fine school is a wonderful chance for any girl."

"No, no, you don't quite understand. It's something special for me! To come to *this* school, to the chateau, that's what I've always wanted."

Cherry wisely remained silent, touching the leaves which brushed the open car window. She knew from her nursing experience the importance of *not* asking questions. But she hoped that Lisette, of her own accord, would tell more. For Cherry sensed an unhappy situation here behind Lisette's carefully chosen phrases, and she would like to help her.

"Do you suppose our driver is *ever* coming back?"

"I forgot to tell you," Lisette said, "that the school station wagon is in the garage for repairs. Maybe we can beg a ride from the driver of that funny little wagon coming up the road."

"But she's heading away from the school," Cherry commented.

A plump, jolly little woman was driving the horse. She wore an old-fashioned sunbonnet; a wide straw hat rested on the horse's head, with holes for his ears to stick through. What captivated Cherry was the waves of flower scent from the wagon which held a few baskets of flowers. As the woman drew up alongside, she called:

"Whoa, Jupiter! Afternoon, young ladies! Is it hot enough for you?"

"We'll have cooler weather soon," Cherry answered. Lisette only managed to smile.

"You're from Mrs. Harrison's school, I'll wager. I'm

Molly Miller from Rivers' Crossing—that's more of a crossroads than a village. Maybe you've heard of me and my flowers? I have a real nice nursery. Been out selling bouquets today."

"I've been admiring them," Cherry said, intoxicated with the rich scents. Most of the baskets were empty but in the remaining bouquets were a bewildering variety of blossoms.

"Mrs. Miller, I've been brought up right here in Illinois," Cherry said, "but I've never seen a home-grown bouquet with so many different kinds of flowers."

"Oh, we pride ourselves around here on our flowers." Molly Miller's weather-beaten face beamed. "Now, this is a specially nice bunch—so many varieties, four kinds of roses, night-scented stock, a few zinnias, asters—"

Abruptly, Lisette leaned across Cherry to inquire, "Are those for sale?"

"Why, certainly, young lady." Molly Miller named a small price. In her eagerness Lisette all but seized the bouquet from her. The farm wife looked pleased.

"Why don't you come over and see my garden and hothouses some day?" she invited them. "It's well worth a trip, if I do say so myself."

Cherry thanked the friendly woman, who gathered the reins tighter and clucked to her horse. As the wagon wheels started to turn, Lisette called out:

"Wait a moment—please! What's the name of this white spray—the one that smells both sweet and tangy? It's an odd scent—"

"Now, young lady," the farm wife called back, "I must hurry home. But you come and visit me—like I told you—" She waved good-by to them and the horse trotted merrily up the road.

Cherry waved back, then turned to Lisette, who was rapturously smelling the bouquet. She had never seen anyone enjoy flowers as much as Lisette.

"Miss Cherry, I didn't mean to—well, snatch the bouquet for myself, you know. I'd like very much to put them in the infirmary. Or at least half of them."

"For the empty beds to enjoy?" Cherry commented, hoping that there were no patients yet. "No, you keep the flowers, Lisette. Thanks, anyway."

"Look at the roses! White, fawn-colored, yellow, and those big red cabbage roses. Don't you love roses? What do you think this strange scent can be?"

Cherry and Lisette went through the bouquet, naming each flower. They were uncertain of one special rose, and unable to identify the silvery-white spray. Whether the odd, lovely odor came from flower or leaf of the silvery spray was a question, too.

Not until they heard gasoline gurgling into the taxi's tank did they notice that their driver was back, dusty and disgusted.

"I'd better git me one of Molly Miller's horses," he said, noticing the bouquet. "Sorry to keep you waitin'."

The taxi started off again. This time, they turned off the main highway and followed side roads. Birds sang on the boughs, a brook bubbled along.

Cherry sat up straighter, inquisitive to see where they were heading. She powdered her nose and straightened her hat, with one eye on the road. Presently she saw the tall, flat roof of a house, half hidden in trees but rising above them.

The taxi followed a gravel driveway which led into large, rather neglected grounds. Several smaller frame buildings stood among the grove of oak trees, but it was the main house which held Cherry's attention.

"It does resemble a chateau!" Cherry exclaimed. The lovely old building, surrounded by gardens, gave an impression of dignity, even stateliness. Its tall, narrow style was more Victorian than French, with arched windows and two small formal entrance porches, at front and side.

"Yes, folks around here used to call it the Chateau Larose," the driver said. He had appointed himself a sort of guide, as the three of them stood before the house, admiring it. "That's to say, they called it that when a private family resided here. Before the school started up in here. That's some years ago."

Cherry turned to Lisette, expecting some natural tie might exist between the girl with the French name and the house of a style transplanted from France. But Lisette remained silent, though a stroke of pink appeared in each ivory cheek.

"I must be mistaken," Cherry thought. "There are French descendants in St. Louis. The French founded the city—and it's in this general area. Perhaps Lisette wanted to see this chateau simply because it *is* French!"

The driver was waiting for his fare. Both girls opened their handbags and Lisette fumbled.

"I'm afraid I didn't bring enough. Or else spent too much—"

"Never mind," Cherry said. "I'll take care of it."

"Maybe I put my change in the inner pocket—" Lisette shook her purse, and as she did so, the bouquet and the heavy book on her arm dropped to the ground. The book fell open. Cherry, who stooped to retrieve it, saw the book snatched away and snapped shut. She was a little surprised at Lisette's haste—as if she did not want Cherry to see what the book was about. Pretending not to notice Lisette's strange action, Cherry picked up the bouquet, then turned to the driver and took care of the fare.

"Thank you very much, Miss Cherry," Lisette said in a small voice. "I'm terribly embarrassed. I'll repay you."

"I'll be embarrassed if you do. I'll tell you what! You may contribute one red rose to the infirmary. Here are your flowers."

Lisette smiled shyly at her as if to say, "I like you." Then, as she stood silently before the house, the girl seemed to forget Cherry, seemed to be in a world of her own. Half to herself she murmured, "Papa and I always dreamed of this old house. Now I'm really here."

Cherry was puzzled. "And you came early to look around?" she said sympathetically.

Lisette turned crimson. She withdrew into herself again and did not reply. Cherry regretted that she had spoken so hastily, though she intended only a friendly interest! Why was Lisette so evasive and touchy?

"Let's go in the house," Cherry said, still puzzled. "I'd like to meet Mrs. Harrison. Will you introduce me?"

Lisette led the way into the house, which was cool and quiet. No one was in the entrance hall. Lisette knocked on the open door of an attractive reception room, and, since no one was there, went on into the huge sitting room which was Mrs. Harrison's office. The room was shaded, the walls were lined with books and photographs. At the desk a golden-haired woman sat writing.

Lisette said quickly, "Mrs. Harrison, here is Miss Cherry Ames," and then the girl vanished.

CHAPTER II

# *House of Roses*

MRS. HARRISON ROSE FROM HER DESK AND HELD OUT her hand to Cherry. She was a beautiful, tall, stately woman.

"I'm so glad that you're here, Cherry Ames. We're all happy to have you as our nurse. My, what rosy cheeks! You'll be an inspiration to all of us for glowing health. I hope that you'll be happy with us at the Jamestown School."

"Thank you, Mrs. Harrison, I know I shall. I've looked forward so much to meeting you." Cherry's mother had told her of Alicia Harrison's graciousness, and she liked her employer at once.

"Sit down, Miss Ames. No, I'm going to call you Cherry, at least unofficially. If I call you Miss Ames in private, you'll know I'm scolding you! It's too bad you were obliged to take the taxi out here. Let's have some iced tea and get acquainted."

Mrs. Harrison put some letters out of sight, pulled a bell cord, and then, linking her arm through Cherry's, led her to a sofa. A maid came in bringing a tray of tea and cookies, and left.

"Now then!" said Mrs. Harrison, serving Cherry. "How is your mother? I haven't seen Edith in several years but we do correspond." She chatted of her old acquaintance, and then began to talk about Cherry's record as a nurse. She mentioned Cherry's excellent references and was pleased especially with Cherry's range of experience. "Imagine being an army nurse! A school may seem rather tame to you after that, but believe me, you're going to need to draw on all your experience."

"In what way do you mean, Mrs. Harrison?" Cherry asked curiously.

"For one thing, you'll have people of many ages to look out for. Our girls range in age from thirteen or fourteen to seventeen, but our instructors are more mature, of course, and some of the domestic staff—maids, cook, man-of-all-work—are quite elderly. You'll meet them later. Only a few of us are here this early. The others will come pouring in very soon, though."

Mrs. Harrison leaned back against the sofa, as if tired, but instantly sat erect again. Cherry waited for her to go on.

"It's only fair to explain to you, Cherry, that being nurse to the students—who will need by far the most of your attention—is sort of a double assignment. It won't be so much a question of medicines and temperatures as, well, being a good psychologist."

"I think I understand."

"Do you?" Mrs. Harrison looked at her with a surprising sharpness. "You aren't so very much older than our students. I wonder if you might not be rather young to be in full charge."

Cherry felt her cheeks burn rosier than ever. Why did so many people consider that because she was young she might not be capable of handling responsibilities?

"I've been in charge of nursing units before, you know," Cherry said politely.

"Yes. You have. That makes a difference." Mrs. Harrison smiled and offered Cherry more cookies. "Well, perhaps your youth will turn out to be an advantage. The girls may feel closer to a nurse who is near their own age. But you will have to maintain a good example for them."

Heavens, had the headmistress heard of some of the scrapes she'd gotten into at Spencer Hospital? Could her mother have mentioned one or two of the more hilarious ones in her letters? Cherry sat still as a mouse, not knowing exactly what to say next.

"You know, Cherry, the quality of your work will reflect on the school. We all love the school—naturally I do—and the girls have a deep attachment for it."

"Mrs. Harrison, I'll do my very best for you and the school," Cherry promised.

"Good, good. Yes, a genuine love—"

The headmistress stared abstractedly at the bookshelves. Her face with its serene beauty clouded over; she was evidently troubled about something. The silence lengthened. Cherry began to feel she ought to excuse herself. Mrs. Harrison must have a great deal of work to do just before the opening of the term. But her employer glanced up and offered her more tea.

"I don't want to overstay, Mrs. Harrison."

"No, don't go. I have some further things to talk over with you—and show you. You'll have to get acquainted with this house."

"Lisette pointed out the garden as we came in." She did not understand why Mrs. Harrison looked amused. "I enjoyed driving in with Lisette. She seems to be an exceptionally nice girl."

Mrs. Harrison answered only a guarded, "Yes, indeed." It was clear that the headmistress could say much more about Lisette. But she merely smiled in her gentle way.

Mrs. Harrison took Cherry on a tour of the downstairs rooms. Old-fashioned folding doors led from the headmistress's office into a large sitting room at the side of the house.

"As you can see, this is still a private-family sort of house," Mrs. Harrison remarked to Cherry. "I thought it would be a pity to remodel, though we have put in extra bedrooms and baths upstairs. Did you see the other buildings when you arrived? The long, low house is a dormitory for some of the older girls. The two nearer buildings have classrooms and our gymnasium and the arts-and-crafts studio. That's everybody's favorite. This sitting room is my own favorite."

What made the big room still more pleasant was the scent of flowers from the garden. Bright patches of roses —white, pinks, reds—showed from the windows, and then Cherry realized that some of the French doors opened onto a conservatory. This glassed-in room could be entered either from the small side porch or from the sitting room. Cherry remarked on its vivid, growing plants.

"That is partly Lisette's handiwork," said the headmistress. "The child is so entranced with the garden that she begged permission to tend the conservatory and to transplant some of the flowers. Garden flowers won't last beyond the first frost, but thanks to Lisette we'll have roses all winter long in the conservatory."

"That takes quite a bit of doing," Cherry said with admiration. "My mother struggles along in winter with green plants in a sunny bay window. Aren't you fortunate to have a conservatory!"

Mrs. Harrison explained that the house had been built about 1885 by a young man who wanted his bride to have "all the latest things." She took Cherry from the sitting room through a roomy pantry into the kitchen. Here the fragrance of flowers gave way to the buttery aroma of something baking. Cherry met "Auntie" Collier, a good-humored Negro woman who cooked and who would co-operate with Cherry whenever a patient needed special foods. Tina, a wiry, gray-haired little maid who doubled as waitress, would help Cherry whenever the nurse needed her, said Mrs. Harrison. After Cherry shook hands with these two pleasant, busy women, Mrs. Harrison said that later she would meet Mrs. Snyder, their housekeeper, and Perry, who was chauffeur, houseman, gardener, and handyman. This staff seemed to Cherry none too large.

There was nothing pretentious about the school, but it definitely had an air of quiet dignity and friendly intimacy. Though the garden was somewhat neglected, this main building was furnished with some lovely antiques. In the dining room on the other side of the house, the mahogany tables and chairs gleamed like satin. A grandfather's clock in the library chimed every quarter hour. Somebody had set bowls of garden flowers on every marble mantel on this floor. The flowers smelled so fresh that Cherry half expected to see bees and butterflies hovering among them. She was looking forward to a walk in the garden itself.

"Shall we go upstairs?"

Mrs. Harrison preceded Cherry up the big staircase, explaining rather apologetically about the infirmary. Suddenly Lisette appeared out of nowhere at the top landing, then vanished. The headmistress was startled.

"I declare, that girl appears to be all over the house! Lisette?"

But she got no answer. Mrs. Harrison gently shook

her head. She opened a door and invited Cherry in.

If Cherry was disappointed when she saw the infirmary, she managed not to show it. The simple room was adequate, but after working with modern hospital equipment, and now to work with three white iron beds, a sink, a scale, one medicine chest, and one laboratory table holding supplies, was quite a contrast. Not even a sterilizer, though Cherry noticed a two-ring electric stove.

Then Cherry reminded herself that if anyone at the school became seriously ill, that person would be taken to a hospital. The infirmary was designed to take care of minor upsets. "Besides," Cherry chided herself, "good nursing never depends on gadgets alone. It requires skill—and ingenuity."

"You see, Cherry, your infirmary is right over my office." Mrs. Harrison showed her the many windows, the pleasant views, at the front and side of the house. "It's a nice huge room, isn't it? At this end is your supply closet. It almost overhangs the conservatory. And over here is your own room."

This was a square, small room off the other end of the infirmary, shaded by huge oak trees. It might have been a capacious dressing room or infant's room, and the big room must once have been a bedroom. Mrs. Harrison confirmed this.

"That's why the infirmary is rather cut up, you see. It was one of the master bedrooms; there were two other master bedrooms as well in this rambling house. The supply closet is here, and I hope it will be convenient for you. I must admit, Cherry, that the bathroom door sticks on damp days. There's extra drawer space in this old chest. You may need it when some new linens I ordered arrive."

For all its inconvenience, Cherry decided, the infirmary was homelike. Perhaps a fireplace and a breeze rippling the branches of the trees would do her patients more good than a sterilizer. There was more than one kind of nursing, as Mrs. Harrison had said earlier.

One all-important question remained.

"Mrs. Harrison, what physician will I work with?"

"Well, the school has been depending on a local man, Dr. Horton Wilcox, for several years now. We do not retain a resident doctor, we don't really need one. Dr. Wilcox lives only three miles away, and he's amiable and has had a lifetime of medical experience. The only thing is, you may sometimes have to— Yes, Mary?" Mrs. Harrison turned. "Were you looking for me?"

A girl stood shyly in the doorway. She was almost Lisette's age and height, but seemed unsure and rather lost here. Mrs. Harrison went over to Mary and put her arm around the girl. She bent her golden head down to the girl's lowered face.

"Why, Mary dear, you mustn't be shy. It's always hard for anyone in a new place, at first. Here's another new friend—our nurse. Mary Gray, Cherry Ames."

Cherry smiled encouragingly at Mary Gray, who was not quite brave enough to meet her gaze. She was almost green with homesickness. Mrs. Harrison explained that Mary was here early because her parents had to make an unexpected trip to the West Coast.

"Mrs. Harrison, may I turn on the radio in the sitting room?" Mary asked. "I—the regulations—I don't understand them very well yet."

"The only regulation is to keep happy and well and make friends, and study. Where's Lisette? Why don't you and Lisette go for a walk across the meadow before supper? There's an old mill that's worth seeing."

"Lisette is reading a book she brought back from the library in town. She's busy."

"That child! Well, never mind. You and I will take the walk to the mill ourselves. Right away, if Miss Cherry will excuse us? Are you ready?"

"Oh, Mrs. Harrison, would you?" Mary came to life. "I'd love that! May I just change my shoes? Excuse me."

She ran out. The headmistress sat down on one of the high, narrow beds.

"You see, Cherry, there's an example of what I was attempting to tell you. Mary is far too quiet, far too shy. It's not a matter for aspirin tablets. I should brief you on others who may give you problems."

She mentioned an older, flamboyant girl named Sibyl "who doesn't *mean* to make trouble." She named Nancy who became sick at the very approach of examinations, so that she was unable to take them. At that moment the voices of Lisette and Mary floated in from the hall.

"Lisette!" Mrs. Harrison summoned her. "Will you

show Miss Cherry the rest of this floor? Mary and I are going outdoors." She turned in the doorway. "Dinner is at six-thirty, Cherry, though it will be supper in this weather. We usually have a stroll in the garden afterward. See you then."

The headmistress went off, with Mary Gray following along like a leggy colt. Cherry was disappointed to see her go, for she wanted to hear about Dr. Wilcox. Turning in a good performance on this new job would depend in part on what Dr. Wilcox required of her.

"Lisette, I don't suppose you've met Dr. Wilcox, have you?"

"I'm so new here, Miss Cherry, that all I really know so far is the house. Would you like to see these upstairs rooms?"

Cherry followed, as Lisette quickly showed her the rooms. After the infirmary came the faculty sitting room, Mrs. Harrison's bedroom, an upstairs study for students, and then several small bedrooms and baths.

"Is there a third floor, Lisette?"

"No, just a few feet of space for air and insulation, I think."

It was useless to ask Lisette questions about other matters. She was scarcely acquainted here. She talked enthusiastically about the old garden and the chateau's stained-glass windows of many colors.

"I love this house," Lisette said with a sigh, as she later helped Cherry unpack. She added quickly, almost defiantly, "Anyone would love it."

It took Cherry the rest of the afternoon to get settled. She hung away her dresses and her crisp white uniforms, and laid out her own thermometers, bandage scissors, glass syringe, and patients' record book on the infirmary table. By the time she showered and changed, it was time for supper.

The evening meal in the quiet dining room was pleasant. With so few persons here, only the long center table was set, with flowers and lighted candles. Mrs. Harrison presided. Mlle. Gabriel, an animated woman in black who taught French and Italian, sat between Mary and Lisette. Cherry was seated beside Mr. Alex North, a calm, judicial, reserved man who taught the sciences. He was so reserved that she was hard put to it to converse with him. Mrs. Harrison kept them all amused with her stories of the first year she operated the school. Everything had gone wrong—part of the roof caved in, a student innocently brought in a case of mumps, and the tennis courts had been ruined in the longest rains in years.

"I remember," Mr. North said wryly. "No one could have had worse luck. But we weathered it."

"Did we?" Mrs. Harrison laughed a little. "I still have misgivings about that roof, even though it was repaired."

"But is it not true," Mlle. Gabriel said in her quick way, "you yourself have told me, even then girls here had the wonderful time? So loyal!"

They laughed and reminisced. Presently, after coffee in the sitting room, all of them went out into the garden for a stroll. Cherry loved being outdoors in the summer dusk. The sky had turned violet blue, and in this light, the colors of the leaves, grass, and flowers were intensified. The red roses glowed almost like live coals and the white roses appeared luminous. Twilight heightened, too, the perfumes of the garden.

"What a delicious place!" Cherry exclaimed.

"But neglected," Mrs. Harrison said. "See how it has gone to seed. This garden has been neglected for years, I'm afraid."

"Whoever planted it, planted well," Mr. North remarked. He ripped a stem open and examined it. "These are old plants."

"Yes, indeed. Well, we are lucky to have Lisette here to take an interest in it."

Lisette flushed, embarrassed. She invited Cherry and Mary Gray to see the many varieties of roses, explaining, "That's why the house was originally called the Chateau Larose."

The roses were truly extraordinary—not even Lisette knew the names of all of them. Nor could anyone identify the silvery-white spray of blossoms. Cherry took a deep breath of their unusual and lingering scent.

"Aren't two or three of these the same flowers we found in Molly Miller's bouquet?"

"I'm not sure." Lisette looked closely at the fawn rose and at the white spray.

Mary suggested shyly, "Why don't you ask Mr. North?" Lisette ran indoors and returned with a silvery flower from Molly Miller's bouquet, to show to Mr. North.

The science teacher did not recognize it either. He ventured a guess that the silvery-white spray was not a native flower. He compared it to other species and went into such detail that Cherry's attention wandered. She found herself looking up at the infirmary windows.

In the rapidly fading light, she thought she saw a window that she had not noticed from indoors. It was a diamond-shaped window of stained glass, the kind that might or might not open.

When, later, she had said good night to the others and come upstairs, Cherry looked for the diamond-shaped window but could not find it. Perhaps, in looking at the window in the first shadows of evening, she might have misjudged its location. She must look again sometime by daylight, purely out of curiosity, when she was in the garden. It was quite a pretty window, with panes of purple, rose, yellow, and green.

"Like a harlequin's tights," Cherry thought, yawning.

She was suddenly so sleepy that she was tempted to go to bed without washing her face. Good nurse that she was, however, she scrubbed her face and teeth before tumbling into bed.

But it was a strange bed, in a strange house, and Cherry could not go to sleep at once. She listened to unaccustomed creaks and gusts of breeze, thinking what a full day it had been. Cherry drowsed, wondering about the diamond window and puzzling over the inconsistent Lisette. Lisette's intense interest in the cultivation of flowers was rather odd and unusual for a girl of her age. The last thing she was aware of was the scent of flowers, deepening with the night.

CHAPTER III

# *Something Is Missing*

RIGHT AFTER LABOR DAY, GIRLS BEGAN TO ARRIVE IN A rush at the Jamestown School. They poured in in ones and twos and threes, traveling together if they were old pupils, but the majority of them were brought by their parents. Laughter and chatter filled the house, and girls overflowed into the dormitory building and on the sunny grounds. Their noisy reunions reminded Cherry of her own festive times with her Spencer Club crowd, though Mr. North referred to them as "the stampede." Mrs. Harrison declared everyone would actually settle down, once classes began. In the meantime, she beamed like a girl herself, introducing all the new people around, including Cherry. The first day or two of the new term resembled a house party, what with comparing snapshots of summer vacations and trying on one another's new clothes and nobly "getting along" with one's assigned roommates.

Not every girl was happy. Cherry suspected that some of the smiles were bravely put on for a front. Cliques began to form. The leaders of inner circles were on the whole too well mannered to leave any girl out—Mrs. Harrison would not have permitted such unkindness. Even Sibyl Martin, who was sophisticated for sixteen and the most glamorous girl in the school, took time out to be sweet to the freshmen. But the going was hard for shy girls, especially for the new students. Of these, Cherry was most concerned about Lisette.

The curious thing was that Lisette herself did not seem at all concerned. If she had been homesick, as little Mary Gray obviously was, or if she had drawn a difficult girl for a roommate, Cherry might have understood, but there seemed to be no reason why Lisette Gauthier should hold herself aloof from the other girls. That was a sure way to make people say, "Who does she think *she* is?" and get herself disliked. Yet Lisette wore a thoughtful, almost sad air. It was not simply unfriendliness, then.

Cherry was tempted to drop a word of warning to her. "I don't want to speak out of turn, though," Cherry thought. "Wish I could understand what's going on in her secretive little head."

Cherry was disturbed by an incident which she witnessed when the first classes were over for the day.

She was so busy putting the infirmary in tiptop working order and getting acquainted with the girls who popped in, that she hardly left the infirmary except for meals. However, she had to consult with the cook about diets for several girls whose weight needed watching. On her way through the sitting room, she glimpsed Lisette puttering in the conservatory. Two girls were with her. Cherry paused to say hello, then listened in disbelief.

"I think you're mean, Lisette," said Betty Taylor, who was as agreeable as she was freckled. "You could at least tell us the name of that flower."

"I told you, I don't know its name." Lisette was barely short of being rude. "Nancy, please give back the trowel. I need it for transplanting. Please!"

Teasingly, Nancy wriggled away and put the trowel on the farthest ledge. Lisette had to walk over to get it. She was devoting all her spare time to bringing indoors several garden plants to protect them from coming autumn frosts. Cherry wished that Lisette would pay more attention to getting off on the right foot with her classmates and making friends.

"Lizzie's in a tizzy," Nancy remarked, and Betty Taylor smiled an impish, freckled grin. "That is Sibyl's opinion of you, if you must know. Lizzie, we forgive you. Come out and knock some balls across the net with us. It's more fun with three than two."

"Sorry, but I'm right in the middle of transplanting these flowers, can't you see?"

"Oh, nuts. A few old flowers aren't so terribly important as all that." Nancy plucked a flower and stuck it in her mouth. "Look, kids, I'm Carmen."

Lisette looked as if she could murder them with pleasure. Cherry decided that if she was going to step in, this was the moment.

"Can you spare a rose for the infirmary? Hello, Carmen." She grinned at Nancy, then at Betty. "Don José, I presume? I'm feeling a bit like Florence Nightingale myself."

"That's a cute nurse's cap," Betty said. "Is it your school cap, Miss Cherry?"

"No, this is the conventional cap. Lisette, if you'd go outdoors with these girls, they might stop calling you Lizzie."

"But, Miss Cherry, I told you I *have* to make this year count! These flowers are important to me. Of course I'd like to play tennis with them—"

And Lisette remained in the conservatory.

Maybe, Cherry thought, she was an unsociable genius, or just plain contrary. Whatever Lisette's basic personality, she was less lighthearted than the other girls. Cherry was puzzled, too, by Lisette's almost slavish devotion to growing flowers.

Her name came up in the faculty sitting room, too. Cherry dropped in there on Thursday evening for a visit and some advice. Mrs. Harrison had requested her to write a set of rules on good health practices for the school paper. Cherry had done so and now wanted the instructors' comments. Everyone said, "Fine," and insisted that the new nurse stay and chat. Cherry was glad of a chance to become better acquainted with the aristocratic and learned woman, Mrs. Curtis, who taught English and literature. As usual, Mlle. Gabriel was knitting and talking, flitting from topic to topic. Mr. Phelps, who taught mathematics, glanced at her over his chess game with Mr. North as if he could not take Mademoiselle too seriously. But she could make Mr. North chuckle, and that was an achievement.

"—so I say afterward, of course in private, to my student, 'My dear child, if you ever visit Paris, never, never try to speak French. Because, *ma petite,* you would break the ears of true Frenchmen. Your accent? Extraordinary!' "

"Did she weep?" asked Alex North. "I keep a blotter handy for female tears." He winked at Cherry.

"Ah, but one student I have, she is a gem! What beautiful French! Do you all know little Lisette Gauthier?"

"The moody one," said Mrs. Curtis.

"The different one," Mlle. Gabriel pounced.

"She is a bright and alert girl," Mrs. Curtis said impartially. "She stands rather apart from the rest, though."

Cherry ventured to say, "Lisette takes a little knowing, don't you think?"

"Ah, yes!" Mlle. Gabriel beamed at her. "Lisette is not all on the surface; she is a serious one. She must read much, particularly in French. She has an unusual command of the French language—yes, yes, Alex, it's true she is of French descent. But she tells me she has never been to France or French Canada. She has stuffed herself with description of the lovely French countryside." Mlle. Gabriel said wistfully, "She pointed out to me a bergamot tree in the garden."

Lisette and her garden! Cherry was about to ask where the rare citrus tree stood, when, from the hall, came a shriek and a crash of someone falling. The instructors rushed to open the door. The nurse sped to the scene of the accident first.

Tina, the elderly maid, evidently had climbed up on a stepladder to change a light bulb, caught her heel in a rung, and now lay twisted in pain on the floor.

"Don't touch her, anyone," Cherry cautioned.

She eased Tina's shoe off and released her foot. With gentle, skilled hands she probed to see whether Tina had had an electric shock, and whether any of her brittle bones were broken. Cherry carefully rolled her over on the floor to unpin Tina's left arm. She must have tried to brace herself, stiff-armed, then fallen on the arm with her entire weight. Under the skin Cherry felt the sharp point of a splintered bone. Tina's forearm was broken.

"It hurts!" Tina moaned. "Oh!"

"There, there, we'll make you comfortable," Cherry murmured. She saw Mr. North and Mademoiselle, watching. "Mademoiselle, will you please telephone for the doctor to come at once?"

The arm was swelling rapidly. Since they must not risk moving Tina until a temporary splint was applied, Cherry hurried into the infirmary. But applying a splint would take time. First she caught up a blanket, chose a mild sedative, and brought it along to Tina with a glass of water.

"This will help the pain, Tina." Cherry administered the sedative and covered her with the blanket, keeping her warm to combat shock. She managed to ease the hovering instructors out of the way, and requested that someone notify Mrs. Harrison. She bent down and smiled encouragingly at her patient.

"Feel better?" The wiry little woman nodded. "If it starts hurting very badly again, tell me. The doctor will be here soon."

Cherry went back to the infirmary and searched in haste for wooden splints; her hands shook. Silly to be tense about her first patient on a new job! She had taken care of fractures before. It was just that working in an unaccustomed, sparsely supplied ward, for a doctor whom she had not yet met, was trying. Her main concern, however, was for her patient. Cherry located splints but they were too short.

Well, she would have to make do with a pillow or blanket, folded rigid. Cherry folded a blanket to many thicknesses, making it long enough to reach beyond Tina's forearm, padded it well with sterile cotton, and returned with it to the hall. Kneeling beside the woman, she put the cotton side next to Tina's arm, and firmly but gently secured the splint to the arm with gauze bandages. Cherry worked fast, and cautiously; she did not want the sharp ends of the broken bone to move and do further damage.

"There! Now it's safe to move you."

Mr. North and Mr. Phelps, at the nurse's direction, carefully picked Tina up. With Cherry holding the splinted arm motionless, the men carried Tina to one of the infirmary beds.

"Now I'm going to make you some hot tea, Tina, and then I want you to sleep."

Half an hour later her patient was dozing. Lisette had heard of the accident and come in to ask Cherry if she could help. She couldn't, but it was thoughtful of her to offer, Cherry thought. The headmistress had looked in and left. Still the doctor had not arrived. Wasn't he coming tonight? Mrs. Harrison had said he had a very full practice. Perhaps Dr. Wilcox would not come until morning.

Cherry was settled in a chair, watching her patient carefully, when very late someone tapped at the infirmary door. Cherry softly went to the door. There stood, to her surprise, a young man.

"I'm Dr. Wilcox," he said.

"*You're* Dr. Wilcox? I beg your pardon—" He looked little older than herself—just about old enough to be an intern, if that. Cherry felt confused. Mrs. Harrison had said that Dr. Wilcox was an elderly man.

"Didn't someone telephone for Dr. Wilcox?" the young man asked. He was, Cherry noticed for the first time, carrying a physician's satchel.

"I'm the new school nurse, Cherry Ames, sir—uh—Doctor." She held the door open for him. She had better observe the medical courtesies, in any case.

"Oh, yes, Mrs. Harrison told me about you on the telephone," the young man said cheerfully. He glanced over at Tina, who was asleep. A little color had returned to her cheeks. "Mrs. Harrison told me a lot of interesting things about you, Miss Cherry Ames."

"Well, she didn't tell me about *you!*" Cherry said impulsively. "I hope you won't think me rude, or presumptuous, Mr.—Dr. Wilcox, but I expected to see a much older man."

The young man grinned. "That's my father. He's Dr. Horton Wilcox and I'm Dr. Alan Wilcox. Just recently completed my internship and my father asked me to assist him. His practice has grown too large for one man. Father is really the school doctor, but I often come over here to help out."

So that was what Mrs. Harrison had started to explain the other day when Mary Gray had interrupted. Cherry felt sure that the students preferred this engaging young man to any other physician. Dr. Alan was so young and vigorous that his presence acted as a tonic. Besides, he had sparks of mischief in his eyes, for all his professional manner. Probably all the girls were half in love with him. Cherry liked him herself and smiled at him. Dr. Alan smiled right back. Then they got down to work.

"The patient seems to be resting comfortably," the young doctor said. He and Cherry moved over to the bedside. "What happened, Miss Ames?"

"A fall resulting in a fracture, Dr. Wilcox. As you see, I put on a temporary splint." Cherry watched anxiously as Dr. Alan very gently examined the splint. She hoped that he approved of what she had done, for she wanted to merit this young man's respect.

He seemed satisfied. He asked what else Cherry had done, and when she reported giving a mild sedative he seemed satisfied about that, too.

"I'm afraid that we'll have to wake our patient."

Cherry did so, took Tina's pulse, which was normal, and bathed her face and hands. While the nurse did this, Dr. Alan opened his kit and laid out his instruments and wooden splints. Cherry rolled over the enamel table for his use and assisted him. Strangers though they were, they worked together smoothly right from the start.

Dr. Alan confirmed that it was a simple fracture. He found Tina in good condition and not uncomfortable. He examined the arm carefully for any break in the skin or any sign of infection, found none, then very, very gently felt the arm to learn approximately what the type (or pattern) of the bone dislocation was. Cherry waited to learn whether he would want Tina

*Cherry watched anxiously as Dr. Alan examined the splint*

taken to the hospital tonight, but Dr. Alan said, "With good nursing care, this can wait until morning."

Tomorrow at the hospital the arm would be X-rayed, Tina would be given an anaesthetic, then the bone would be manipulated and set into place, and finally a plaster cast put on the arm to immobilize it while the bones knit. For now, Dr. Alan cradled the broken arm in a sturdy wooden splint which was gauze-covered. Cherry bandaged this splint into place.

"Getting tired, Tina?" Dr. Alan patted her free hand. "Try to have a good, long sleep. Nurse Ames will put you into bed and give you a warm drink. More mild sedation as she needs it, Nurse. I'll write out instructions. I'll come back tomorrow, about nine. And, Tina, don't worry about how soon you'll be able to work again. I'll explain to Mrs. Harrison."

Doctor and nurse withdrew to the far end of the big room for instructions about Tina and a few moments of discussion.

"You're a very good nurse, Miss Ames."

"Thank you, Dr. Wilcox."

"You'd better call me Dr. Alan. Everybody does, so as not to confuse me with my father." He grinned easily. "In that case, don't you think I could call you Miss Cherry?"

"I think it could be arranged, Doctor."

"I wish I had a good nurse like you to help me out with my other patients in emergencies." He explained that he could not afford a nurse of his own yet. "Do you suppose Mrs. Harrison could spare you occasionally? It's awfully hard, way out here in the country, to get an R.N., and in serious cases—"

Cherry understood him. "If it's an emergency, yes. I would be willing to ask Mrs. Harrison for permission to leave the school grounds. Of course I can't predict what she'd say. I do have to be available here at all times," Cherry said responsibly, "or at least not far away."

He looked impatient. "We'd only be in this immediate area and my car can make plenty of speed when necessary. What I mean is—if Mrs. Harrison could let you go, and she's always considerate—would you be willing to help me?"

"I'd like to very much!"

"Fine," he said. "Good night, Miss Cherry. I'm really awfully glad to know you."

Cherry watched his tall, husky figure disappear quietly down the staircase, and admitted that she was pretty pleased to meet Dr. Alan herself.

Next morning Cherry fed Tina breakfast, left her in Mademoiselle's care, and since Tina's condition was good, went down to breakfast herself. When the girls heard that the young physician would be coming in to see Tina, there was a great deal of excited chatter. The gayest laughter came from Sibyl Martin's table.

The older girls were always laughing and whispering knowingly, Cherry noticed, with Sibyl the focus of their admiring eyes. This morning she wore a bright yellow sweater which emphasized her red-gold hair. Cherry had to admit Sibyl had style, in a flamboyant way. Half a dozen semiprecious bracelets dangled on her wrist as she gestured. Her family, Mrs. Harrison had told Cherry, doted on her and gave their youngest daughter anything her capricious heart desired. Sibyl had not stopped by the infirmary as yet, so Cherry went over to her table for a moment to introduce herself.

"I'm the new nurse, and you're Sibyl Martin, aren't you? I'd so much rather meet you girls *outside* the infirmary."

Sibyl certainly could be charming. "Have you time to sit down, Miss Cherry, and have another bite with us? We've all been longing to know you—this is Cora, and Francie, and Susan—" The girls smiled and looked very carefully at Cherry's well-cut uniform and dark curls. "We decided you're—oh, dear, I shouldn't say *cute,* should I? But our last nurse was a bore. So *fat.* Ugh."

Cherry chattered for a few minutes, then stopped in for a moment at Mrs. Harrison's office. As usual it was full of flowers from the garden. The headmistress was already busily at work at her desk.

"Oh, good morning, Cherry! How are you this fine morning? How is our poor Tina?"

"Tina is resting well, Mrs. Harrison—" Cherry reported on Tina and on Dr. Alan's visit and arrangements to take Tina to the hospital. She did not think this was the right moment to mention his request for the school nurse to aid him occasionally. She did mention that Dr. Alan recommended buying a small sterilizer for the infirmary but, surprisingly, Mrs. Harrison said it was out of the question. Cherry wondered why —the school put on few frills but seemed comfortably off. Mrs. Harrison murmured about "repairs for this old house." Cherry did not press; she would simply have to improvise.

"Dr. Alan will be here at nine this morning, Mrs. Harrison."

"I want to talk with him myself, I think."

"Yes, Mrs. Harrison."

Before time for his visit, Cherry helped her patient to dress for the drive to the hospital. She expected that Dr. Alan would arrive in his car, not an ambulance, in this case. Then Cherry read over her patient's chart, to make sure it was complete for her report to the doctor, glad that Tina's TPR (temperature, pulse, respiration) were normal, and gave Tina a midmorning glass of orange juice. From the infirmary they heard a car pull up in the driveway. It was exactly nine o'clock.

A minute later Dr. Alan tapped on the infirmary door and entered. Cherry rose.

"Good morning," he said, all business. "How's our patient this morning?" He smiled at Tina, then Cherry.

Cherry made her report, out of the patient's earshot, and gave him the chart. Dr. Alan asked a question or two, then said, "Very good."

"Mrs. Harrison would like to see you, Doctor."

While he went downstairs to talk to the headmistress, Cherry gently helped Tina down the stairs, supporting her a little. As Dr. Alan emerged quickly from Mrs. Harrison's office, Cherry assisted the patient into the waiting car.

"Thanks, Miss Cherry," he said. "We'll have Tina back here in a jiffy—I'll instruct you then."

The car moved off, and Cherry watched them go with a small sense of disappointment. There had been no chance to get better acquainted with Alan Wilcox on this visit. But it was ridiculous to feel disappointed! After these busy hours, Cherry felt at loose ends, that was all.

"What shall I do with my precious free hour?"

She decided to explore the house a bit. Classes were in session, and, except for a few girls who were studying in the upstairs students' room, almost everyone was in the other buildings. The old house was quiet.

Cherry paused beside the grand staircase, noting a closed door up there on the halfway landing—a closet perhaps. She paused to listen to footsteps running up some other flight of stairs. She suspected that, like many an old mansion, this house had concealed stairways, hidden rooms, and deep, secret cellars. Her nose for mystery had led her into many adventures, but never into an old house like this one.

The chiming of the grandfather's clock led her into the library. The room seemed to be empty, but when Cherry turned around an instant later, she saw Lisette kneeling behind a table, her ear pressed to the wall.

"Lisette! What are you doing?"

Lisette was just as startled to see Cherry.

"I—I'm looking for something I dropped—a pencil," she said lamely.

"Haven't you a class?"

"This is my study hour, Miss Cherry. You won't report me, will you?"

"Of course not! But what were you—?"

Lisette fled. Cherry stood there with her mouth open, watching the girl streak up the stairs. She must be headed for the students' room, where she belonged during a study hour.

A dropped pencil indeed! Lisette had not carried notebook or pencils with her, in fact, no books at all. Cherry scanned the wall and the floor where Lisette had been searching, but saw nothing unusual. What was the girl looking for? Or rather, had she been *listening* for something?

Cherry thought about Lisette several times in the next day or two. She had glimpses of that pale face framed in its dark cloud of hair, that small stubborn figure moving aloof from the noisy merriment of the other girls. Lisette took no part in the samba line which started one morning in the shower room, nor would she play charades in the evening on the lawn, and even at mealtimes she did not laugh with the other girls at her table. "She thinks we're idiots," Nancy said cheerfully.

Cherry was not so sure. She thought Lisette looked rather wistfully at the other girls at times. Then why didn't she try to make herself agreeable, instead of wandering away into the garden or conservatory?

The other girls resented Lisette's aloofness. Because of it, trouble flared up Sunday evening, right outside the infirmary door.

Cherry had left the door open. Sunday evening was a pleasant relaxed time, after a week end of seeing family and friends at the school. Bursts of talk drifted in to Cherry about "Isn't he the dreamiest?" and "I could have *died* in my old blue," and "What a cake!" More sophisticated remarks came from Sibyl Martin and her clique, as they loitered on the stairs. "Oh, don't be so romantic. For a boy who's really been around, I think he's terribly—" Cherry could not hear Sibyl finish the sentence, for it was whispered. A gale of laughter followed. The other girls asked Sibyl excited, muffled questions. Some mischief was afoot, probably with Sibyl the center of it.

A cluster of girls moved past the infirmary doorway. Sibyl called out sharply, "Lisette! Where are you going in such a hurry?"

Cherry knew that Lisette's room was on this floor, hers and another newcomer's. So was Sibyl's room.

"Lisette! You took my bracelet, didn't you? The lapis lazuli one." Sibyl said calmly, "Come on, Lisette Gauthier, I don't think it's a very funny joke."

Cherry saw Lisette stop in surprise.

"I don't know what you're talking about, Sibyl."

"I'm afraid you do. I wish you'd return my bracelet. My family gave it to me and it is quite valuable."

"I didn't take it. I don't take other people's things. Don't you dare accuse me falsely!" Lisette cried.

"Falsely? You snoop around this house a lot. Everybody knows it."

There was absolute silence. No answer came from Lisette; she did not deny that she had been prowling.

Cherry was appalled, and sorry for Lisette. A new girl was no match for Sibyl. Lisette had to fight her own battles, right or wrong, but it was hard to believe this strangely serious girl would steal. No, it was not like Lisette, as far as Cherry knew her. But the way Lisette wandered through the house was incriminating, at least on the surface.

Cherry was not surprised when Lisette came into the infirmary late that same evening, complaining of a headache. Her eyes were watery, as if she had been crying. She insisted it was only a cold.

"I must have caught it in the garden last night," she added.

"What were you doing out in the garden at night? You know there's enough dew to be really damp."

"I've been going out nearly every night—rules or no rules—to see the night-scented stock. You know they give their fragrance only at night. They smelled wonderful!" Lisette said, sniffling. "Especially last night."

Had Lisette only been in the garden last night? Had

she also been in Sibyl's room? Sibyl had been out to the village movie with Cora and Francie last evening, Cherry heard, but she kept her question to herself.

"Hold still while I take your pulse and temperature. Why, Lisette! You're really ill. I'm going to keep you in here for the night."

Lisette, usually so self-willed, did not argue. She obediently went down the hall to her room and returned in a few minutes bringing nightgown and robe. She seemed relieved to have Cherry tuck her into one of the crisp, cool beds. Cherry gave her an aspirin tablet with a glass of orange juice, brought from the kitchen, and placed a light blanket on the bed.

"We'll nip that cold in the bud." She did not tell Lisette that she probably had flu. "Extra rest is the best way. Comfortable?"

"Yes, Miss Cherry." Yet Lisette continued to sit up against the pillows, robe drawn around her thin shoulders. Cherry did not insist that she lie down at once. Patients sometimes wanted to talk.

Cherry sat down in the armchair and waited, making herself busy with the patient's chart.

"Miss Cherry? Are you writing about me?"

"Yes. Your temperature, pulse, respiration, and so on, to show the doctor when he comes to see you tomorrow."

"What do you write down under 'and so on'?" Lisette giggled but could not keep up the pretense.

There was a pause.

"Don't you want to lie down now?"

"No. Miss Cherry? May I ask you a crazy sort of favor?"

Cherry thought Lisette was going to mention the missing bracelet, and said, "Of course."

"I wish very much that you'd bring me some of those garden flowers. Please? I'll tell you *exactly* the ones I want—a silver spray, a sprig of stock, the fawn roses but only one or two, and a China rose—"

Cherry started to smile at this exorbitant fondness for flowers. Then she saw the intent expression in Lisette's eyes. The girl's passion for flowers was extraordinary! Cherry felt almost troubled.

"Would you get them for me? Please?"

"Yes, I'll get them for you first thing in the morning."

Lisette was at last content, and slept.

## CHAPTER IV

# *Secret Journal*

CHERRY WAS DELIGHTED WHEN ONE MORNING A FAT letter arrived from No. 9, in New York's Greenwich Village, the Spencer Club's now-and-then headquarters. Gwen and Vivian wrote the letter together, reporting on what their fellow nurses were doing. Considering how very close together they all had been during their training at Spencer Hospital, Cherry thought, they certainly were flung far apart now. Gwen and Vivian were continuing their nursing jobs in New York, Bertha Larsen was visiting her folks at the farm, Ann Evans was very married and taught a first-aid class for her community's Girl Scouts. Mai Lee was en route from one nursing assignment to another, and had promised to write. The girls were eager to know if Cherry enjoyed being a boarding school nurse.

To tell the truth, Cherry was a bit lonesome. She

had only one patient to care for, since Tina was able to be up now. The teachers were too old and staid to be companionable. The students were too young—not exactly too young, but Cherry was expected to be on her professional dignity. One bright spot was young Dr. Wilcox who came to treat Lisette's flu, which had lasted almost a week now. They could not visit much, but it was good to have him come in.

Lisette was very quiet. Even when the girls from her classes were allowed to visit her, she was not disposed to talk. It was reticence, not illness, Cherry knew, which kept her silent. Just the same, Lisette's face lit up at seeing Nancy and shy Mary Gray, and Bea who was tall and growing taller by the day.

"Miss Cherry, do you think Bea will ever stop growing?"

"Gee, I'm five-ten already. The king-size kid."

"Lisette, you missed irregular verbs in Latin today and are you lucky! All that junk that's never going to do us any good. You're lucky—no books or classes."

Lisette merely smiled and offered them her box of cookies. She did not say she had a thick book under her pillow. She did not tell Mlle. Gabriel, either, who was a devoted visitor.

"*Chérie,* French 4 is a sad class without its best pupil. Do you know how Sue translated today? She read, 'The soup is under the uncle!' " She chuckled and so did Lisette.

Mrs. Curtis looked in to say hello, and so did Mr.

North. The most faithful visitor was the headmistress herself. Cherry would have been touched by Mrs. Harrison's daily visits except that she was so strict with Lisette.

"I haven't wanted to talk to you until you felt stronger, Lisette, about something which disturbs me very much."

Mrs. Harrison's sea-blue eyes were kind but stern at the same time. Lisette listened carefully and, standing beside the bed, so did Cherry.

"I am aware, whether you thought I knew it or not, of your frequent wanderings around the house and garden. I have noticed it myself, and I have heard one or two persons comment on it."

*Has Sibyl talked?* Cherry held her breath, waiting for Mrs. Harrison to mention the missing bracelet.

"I am anxious to hear your explanation, Lisette, as to why I have twice found you on the wrong floor when you had no reason for being there."

Lisette hesitated. "I'm sorry, Mrs. Harrison. I only wanted to explore this old house."

"But why, Lisette?" The girl plucked at the blanket. Mrs. Harrison waited. "At first I thought you had been punished enough already by contracting this cold or flu in the damp garden. But you make it necessary for me to impress on you that you have no special privileges at the school."

"But, Mrs. Harrison, I never expected any special privileges!"

"Then we understand each other. I wish you'd think a little more about why you are here. It's to get an education, Lisette, and to make friends. Please don't dream this year away. It's your big year. Mlle. Gabriel and Mr. North tell me that you do excellent work in their classes."

"Did they? I'm so glad."

"So am I. You could do just as brilliantly in your other courses, if you'd pay attention. I must impress this on you, Lisette. That's why I am withdrawing your free Saturday afternoons for a while."

Cherry waited for Lisette to promise that she would not prowl or explore again. But the girl made no such statement. At any rate, she would not lie.

"I'm not doing anything bad, Mrs. Harrison. Please believe me. Will you have to write to my mother about this?"

"No, I don't think so," the headmistress said gently. "We won't worry her now, but will hope you'll remember the rules."

Mrs. Harrison left the infirmary. Cherry glanced at her patient. Any other girl probably would have been close to tears, or fired to do better. Not Lisette. She looked determined and defiant.

"My big year! As if I didn't know."

"Losing your free Saturdays is too bad." Cherry wondered if the headmistress was not disciplining Lisette more severely than necessary. Something complex existed here, Cherry sensed.

"Yes, losing my Saturdays is a shame, but it's worth it." Lisette did not expand on this. Instead she let out a big sigh. "I'm so glad Mrs. Harrison didn't bring up the question of Sibyl's bracelet. Do you suppose she knows?"

"That's a hard question. Maybe she wants you and Sibyl to settle the matter peaceably between yourselves."

"I'd hate Mrs. Harrison to think that I stole anything. Stole! It weighs on me, Miss Cherry."

"I don't think that she knows about the bracelet."

Lisette cheered up. Better morale meant better health.

Cherry felt rewarded for her nursing efforts by seeing her patient nearly well. She still felt concern for Lisette, though, in the troubling business of the bracelet.

She was fairly convinced by now that Lisette had nothing to do with the missing trinket. Sibyl might be pampered and flighty, but not so malicious as to trump up a false charge. But how to clear Lisette of the charge? The best way might be to consult Sibyl herself, and get as much information about the bracelet as possible.

A crowd of girls clustered around Sibyl as usual at lunch on Thursday. Cherry waylaid her as they all were leaving the dining room. She asked Sibyl to come into the library for a few minutes' talk.

"It's about the bracelet," Cherry said.

"Oh! You've found it! Cheers! Cora, Francie, my bracelet's been returned—" she called after them.

"Now, now, don't leap to conclusions," Cherry said

with a smile. "Sibyl, you know Lisette has been under my observation for nearly a week, and I honestly don't believe she took your bracelet. Do you think there's a chance that it might be mislaid?"

"Really, Miss Ames! I'm not such a goop."

"Of course not. But are you certain it hasn't slid down behind something in your room? Perhaps when the room was cleaned? Lisette feels dreadful about the incident."

"She ought to." Sibyl touched her red-gold hair.

"*Please* co-operate with me. I don't think you're the kind of person who'd deliberately hurt another girl," Cherry said.

Sibyl's insolent expression changed to bewilderment. "I'm not trying to hurt Lisette. All I want is my bracelet. I'm not accustomed to being treated shabbily." She bridled. "Anyway, I'm not hurting Lisette."

"Not on purpose, I'm sure."

"Those plain-looking girls are always jealous. Just because I'm popular. Oh, well, what do you think I ought to do? I've searched for it for *days!*"

"When did you wear the bracelet last?"

"Last Saturday night when I went out with Freddie. Oh!" Sibyl's hands flew to her lips. Her eyes widened. "I didn't mean that."

On that evening Sibyl was supposed to have been at the village movie with some other girls.

Cherry knew the school did not permit its girls to

have unchaperoned evening dates. So Sibyl had fibbed and slipped away with Freddie! This secret dating must be why Cora and Francie and the rest were always giggling and fluttering about Sibyl.

"You won't tell on me, Miss Cherry?" Sibyl coaxingly took her hand.

"N-no, I won't report you," Cherry promised uneasily. She hated being a carrier of tales. She had no wish to get Sibyl into trouble with the headmistress. It would do much more good if she could prevail upon Sibyl not to go out alone with Freddie, whoever he was, again. "You know, Sibyl, the rule about no dating may be tiresome, but it's for your own protection."

"Mrs. Harrison makes rules that were dandy for when she was a girl! I can take care of myself, thanks."

Cherry bit her lip. "Freddie knows about the rule, doesn't he? Doesn't he care that he's going to get you into a jam at school?"

"No one is scared of a few silly rules. Didn't you ever break a few yourself?" Cherry colored slightly. "Honestly, why should I sit here when Freddie can show me a gorgeous time?"

"Is Freddie about your age?"

"He's eighteen. Do you want to know where he's taking me next time? To the Golden Door Inn! Where they have big-name bands and they give prizes of French costume jewelry to the best dancers. Maybe I'll win." She stood up. "Tell you about it, maybe—"

Sibyl flounced out. Cherry sat there, troubled. When

she went upstairs, she was sure of one thing—with a flighty girl like Sibyl, the bracelet could be carelessly lying somewhere out of sight in her room.

When Cherry reached the infirmary, the door was closed. It was always left a little ajar. She was annoyed—Lisette was the only one in there, and she was supposed to be in bed.

"Why did you close the door?" Cherry asked. "You shouldn't have gotten up."

Lisette looked startled. "I was just—er—looking for something."

Again! Cherry gave a quick, sweeping look around the infirmary and into her own room. Everything was in its usual place.

"May I have a fresh pillowcase, Miss Cherry?"

Cherry brought a pillowcase and went over to the bed. Lisette hastily took a thick book from under her pillow and slid it under the covers.

"What a secretive pussycat you are!"

"Dr. Alan did give me permission to read, Miss Cherry."

"It must be an awfully interesting book, the way you treasure it. Isn't that the same book I saw you reading on the train?"

"Mm-hmm." Lisette did not volunteer the title. Cherry noticed that Lisette had covered it in plain wrapping paper, so that its title did not show, although, since it was a library book and library books were often soiled, she might have covered it for cleanliness.

"Lisette, do you want to hear about a talk I had with Sibyl a few minutes ago?"

"Oh, yes!"

Cherry described what had been said. Nothing, really, had been accomplished. Lisette's face fell.

"I suppose Sibyl will believe me guilty until I prove I'm innocent. Only I don't know how. Suppose she tells Mrs. Harrison!"

Cherry felt almost as troubled as Lisette. It did not console the girl to say, "I'll try to think of a way to clear you." When suppertime came, Lisette was too miserable to eat.

"Would you like some flowers, Lisette? There are still quite a lot left in the garden."

She sent one of the girls for a few roses and the fragrant silver spray. Lisette brightened; her whole mood cleared. "She's a strange, changeable girl," Cherry thought.

By Saturday Lisette was well enough for Cherry to take the morning off. She had errands and shopping to do, and since almost the entire school was in flourishing health, Mrs. Harrison said Cherry might go to Riverton.

On the train Cherry was pleased to bump into Dr. Alan. It was the first time he had seen her in anything but a white uniform—this morning she wore a red sports dress, and a ribbon to tie back her curls. Alan took a good, long, appreciative look.

"Do you always glow like this first thing in the morning? Now that you're out of uniform, Miss Cherry, I can tell you I'd like to know you in a nonprofessional capacity, too."

"Then we can't mention anything medical now, can we?"

But within two minutes they were talking away enthusiastically about Dr. Alan's interning experiences and Cherry's previous job.

"We're like the busman on a holiday who goes for a bus ride." Cherry laughed.

"Well, we have plenty to say to each other." The train was pulling into town. "What about meeting me for lunch after we've both done our errands?"

But there was no time for that today. Cherry and Dr. Alan parted, knowing comfortably that they'd meet soon again at the school. She was glad she'd worn her red dress.

Cherry's most important shopping, after a flurry of small purchases such as tooth powder and hair clips for Nancy, was to find a birthday present for her mother, so Cherry was looking for an especially nice gift. Riverton was a fair size town and its broad streets were lined with smart shops.

Yet she found nothing in the shopwindows which her mother did not already have—scarf, purse, gloves, perfume. On a side street Cherry noticed a sign, "Antique Jewelry," and walked down to look at the shop. Portrait miniatures, massive old gold chains, garnet brooches, and seed-pearl earrings gleamed on the velvet trays. "Must be expensive," Cherry thought. She moved toward the side of the window where a small card read: "Anything on This Tray, Five Dollars." She could easily afford five dollars. Then she saw it!

At first Cherry was not sure. She looked at the dark-blue mottled stones, at the dull gold links joining them, and tried to remember whether this was one of the bracelets she had seen dangling from Sibyl Martin's wrist.

"Well, one way to find out is to ask questions."

The man who waited on her, an unhurried elderly man, was the proprietor of the shop.

"Yes, miss, these stones are lapis lazuli. Very popular about thirty, forty years ago. I wouldn't call the bracelet a real antique. A semiantique."

The bracelet could have belonged to Sibyl's mother or grandmother, then.

"Would you mind telling me, sir, where you obtained this bracelet?"

"Not at all. A young man brought it in about a week ago. Yes, on a Monday afternoon. He was anxious to sell it. Needed cash, he said."

"Needed cash?" Cherry echoed.

"Yes. He wanted to take his best girl to the Golden Door Inn. Told me all about it—how this would help pay for some of it. He fancied himself quite the gay young blade, that boy."

"Did he tell you his name?" Cherry asked.

The proprietor shook his head.

"Well, I think I'll buy it," Cherry decided. It might or might not be Sibyl's; the chance was worth the investment.

The man started to put the bracelet in tissue paper in a silver-paper box. Cherry interrupted him.

"Just a minute! Has that box a label on it? I want a label, please, showing the name and address of this shop."

It would be proof of where Sibyl's bracelet had gone to, if Cherry were on the right track. The man found a label for her and stuck it on the lid of the box.

"Can I show you something else, miss? I acquired some handsome enamel flower pins from an estate this week—"

She had almost forgotten the present for her mother! The enameled pansy of purple and yellow would appeal to her mother, who took pride in her bed of pansies. Then, clutching her two precious purchases, Cherry lunched on a sandwich and a glass of milk at the station, ran for the train, and arrived back at the Jamestown School in the early afternoon.

In the sleepy warmth of a mid-September Saturday afternoon, the chateau and its grounds were deserted. Most of the girls had gone off, the seniors to shop and the younger ones on a hike. Only two others, who, like Lisette, had forfeited their Saturday privileges, were on the porch. Cherry found Lisette dressed and shakily sitting on the conservatory steps, in the sun.

"Lean over toward me," Cherry said in a low voice. "I have something rather confidential to show you."

She undid the silver-paper box and gave Lisette a glimpse of the bracelet.

"Is it Sibyl's?" Lisette whispered.

"Not sure, but I think so," Cherry answered.

"Cherry—I mean, Miss Cherry—where did you find it? You don't know what a relief this is to me! I feel as if you're rescuing me from some awful fate."

"Well, I was trying."

Lisette threw her arms around Cherry and hugged her. "I felt all along that you were my friend. Now I *know* it!"

Cherry, too, felt closer friends now. She told Lisette that "some man" had brought the bracelet to the antique shop. She did not feel it fair to divulge that the "man" was probably Sibyl's date, Freddie.

"How do you suppose the man happened to have the bracelet?" Lisette asked. "Do you think Sibyl lost it and he found it?"

"It's a fair guess," Cherry said wryly. "Only Sibyl can answer that."

During the afternoon she debated going to the headmistress with the bracelet and decided it was too drastic, not necessary. A nicer way would be to show the bracelet to Sibyl first, and give her a chance to say what had taken place. She found Francie, one of Sibyl's friends, shampooing her hair.

"Is Sibyl around? Or coming back for dinner?"

"Didn't you hear, Miss Cherry? She's gone home for a few days to attend her sister's wedding. Sibyl's going to be maid of honor, and she has the most gorgeous dress!"

Inwardly Cherry chafed at the delay in settling the matter of the bracelet. She hoped Sibyl would not squeeze in another date with Freddie on her way back to school. Certainly his character was questionable. But at the moment Cherry was more concerned with Lisette's problem—the accusation of theft. Until Sibyl returned, she could not be cleared.

Late that night Cherry wondered if her concern for Lisette was warranted.

It was to be Lisette's last night in the infirmary, so Cherry, half asleep in her adjoining room, did not bother to get up when she heard Lisette get out of bed and tiptoe around the room. Probably she wanted a glass of water. Then Cherry heard a soft, strange, persistent tapping. The sound seemed to come not from the floor but from a wall somewhere.

Cherry listened, waiting in the dark for Lisette to return to bed. When that did not happen, Cherry got up, slipped on her robe, and entered the infirmary. She snapped on the light.

Lisette looked out of the big supply closet. Her hand was still upraised—arrested in the act of tapping the wall. She stammered, "Now you're really going to be angry with me."

"I certainly am going to scold you for your behavior!

No wonder you are suspected of theft when you go prowling like a thief!"

"I'm not a thief!" Lisette wailed.

"What's the use of my trying to clear you when you go creeping around like this at night? This afternoon you said we're friends and now I find you—"

"We *are* friends," Lisette choked out. "I'm not deceiving you. I'm only searching for something."

"At midnight? What for?"

Lisette wiped her eyes and blew her nose. "Please let's turn out the ceiling light, or someone will notice and come in and ask questions."

Cherry darkened the room, leaving only the night light burning. Lisette paced up and down.

"You don't have to tell me anything," Cherry reminded her, more gently. "It's just that I want my patients to behave themselves in the infirmary."

"I already told you about what it's like at home!" Lisette burst out. She talked rather incoherently of her mother's financial straits and her long-time desire to come to this school. "And now that I'm here, I won't let anyone stand in my way! Not even you, Cherry."

"*I* stand in your way? Why, surely you can see I've been trying to help you."

Lisette stopped her pacing. "Yes, you're very patient with me. You're the only person in this whole school who's really and truly my friend."

"I think Mrs. Harrison, who gave you a scholarship,

is your friend. So is Mlle. Gabriel, and Nancy and Mary—"

"I can't tell *them* anything. They'd laugh at me." The girl studied Cherry. "You said just now you want to help me. Do you really mean it?"

Cherry nodded. Lisette sat down. Cautiously, she confided that this house was originally her great-grandfather's, who came from France.

"That's why I'm a little—well—sad about the Chateau Larose. The other girls think I'm snobbish, but it's not that."

Cherry did not understand what there was to feel sad about. Lisette gave a shaky laugh.

"You know what? This big infirmary used to be one of the master bedrooms. For all I know, it may have been my great-grandfather's bedroom. I asked Mrs. Harrison but she didn't know." She began talking rapidly. "Don't you think it's striking that I should be overlooking the very same garden he describes in his journal?"

"So he left a journal! In French? What else did he write about?"

Lisette looked as if she could bite her tongue for letting mention of his journal slip out.

"Oh, nothing much," she said, elaborately casual. Then she admitted, "I brought the journal to school with me. Nobody knows it's here except you—and except my mother, of course."

"Is that the book you keep under your pillow?"

"N-no. It isn't a regular book, just a sort of old diary—"

A wave of scented air blew in from the garden. Cherry asked, "Did your great-grandfather plant the garden originally?"

"Yes, he did." Lisette seemed to be indulging in one of her dreams again, then said earnestly:

"You see, Cherry, there's a secret concealed somewhere in this old house and I must find it. I must! There isn't much time."

"Wha-a-at? Does Mrs. Harrison know about this?"

"No, and I don't want to worry her. Cherry, you said you'd help me."

Cherry hesitated. She would not fail Lisette, but she could not rush heedlessly into a fantastic-sounding situation. *A secret concealed somewhere in this old house.* Well, perhaps some sort of secret lingered here. The important thing was that Lisette wanted so urgently to search for it, and was asking Cherry's help. There returned to Cherry the headmistress's comment to her on her arrival at the chateau: that much of her nursing would be applied psychology. Perhaps now, with Lisette, understanding would benefit the girl more than further medication. Perhaps here was the nurse's opportunity to draw Lisette out of her secretiveness and strangeness. All this went through Cherry's mind in a flash. She said:

"Of course I want to help you, you know that. But naturally I'd like to know what I'd be getting into."

Lisette answered guardedly. "Well, the first thing we must find is a doll. That's our first step."

"A doll! Lisette, are you running a fever again?" Cherry said, half laughing.

"I'm serious. It's a doll that dates from my great-grandfather's time, it's hidden somewhere in this house. And it *is* a secret."

Cherry felt doubtful about embarking on a secret search, without Mrs. Harrison's knowledge or permission, for a doll which might or might not exist. Had there even been such a doll? If so, could it actually still be in the chateau after four generations? Could a doll have survived different tenants, including a school, and all the moving of furniture, all the years of house cleaning? Wouldn't the chance of finding anything so perishable as a doll be pretty remote? Cherry asked Lisette these things, tactfully.

"We *can* find the doll," Lisette insisted. "I believe that because the journal refers quite definitely to a hidden doll. Do you know what I think? Maybe great-grandfather hid it well, so that it's still safe."

"We-ell, maybe. It could be like searching for a needle in a haystack. But you haven't told me *why* we must find this doll."

"Because," Lisette said, struggling to remain patient, "the doll holds the clue to what I'm here at the chateau for! Please, won't you take my word that it's important? I tell you, Cherry, everything depends on finding the doll—"

" 'Everything'? If finding the doll is only the first step, what's your ultimate goal? Can't you tell me?" Cherry urged. "If I trust you, won't you trust me, too?"

Even now Lisette was reluctant to confide too much of her secret. From her expression Cherry thought she was going to withdraw again into her aloofness and moodiness, and Cherry did not want that to happen, having made this much progress with her. Lisette said:

"I wish you'd trust me and just take my word for it."

Cherry drew a deep breath. In her heart she did trust this girl, and had never been given any reason to mistrust her.

"All right, you don't have to tell me everything right away. I said I'd help you. I'll keep my word."

"Will you keep mum, too?"

Cherry nodded. Lisette smiled at her in relief. Now they were almost conspirators.

CHAPTER V

# *Search for the Doll*

CHERRY WAS SO BUSY THE EARLY PART OF THE WEEK—Jannie was in isolation with a septic sore throat—that she had no chance to search for the doll. She had not even been able to make plans for a search when she received a message that the headmistress would like to see her in her office at three o'clock.

In a spanking fresh white uniform, Cherry arrived in the anteroom, congratulating herself. She was not only on time—she was five minutes early. She sat down and then noticed through the anteroom door that Mrs. Harrison had a visitor—a man seated with his back to Cherry.

"I'm not an ogre, you know, Alicia. I'm *obliged* to warn you in a friendly way that they won't wait much longer—"

Cherry did not want to eavesdrop, so she rose and

started out of the anteroom, but Mrs. Harrison called to her:

"Please stay! Do sit down."

Reluctantly Cherry resumed her place. The headmistress *could* close the door if she wanted to. Cherry tried not to listen but she could not help hearing.

"Now, Alicia, when you first started making delayed payments on this mortgage, the bank didn't bother you too much. They took my word for it, as an old friend of your family and in my capacity as a bank official, that you were a good risk."

"I realize that I've frequently been slow with the payments," Mrs. Harrison murmured.

"Not merely slow. You've fallen too far behind. And now that these Riverton people want to buy the chateau and grounds, I can't intercede for you much longer. The bank wants to sell. This land is valuable and those people are making a very attractive offer."

"It would be the end of the school! The end of my livelihood, too. But, Ralph, I can't make a payment right now. You know I'm pinched financially. The costs of overhead have gone up. If the enrollment were larger— This summer I had to put in a new heating unit, too." Mrs. Harrison sighed. "What am I to do?"

"I wish I knew, Alicia. I only wish I knew how to advise you or help you."

"I've put so much into this school! Not only money and work, but hope—love—"

Cherry could see how distressed the headmistress

was. She did not want to hear any more. She slipped out into the entrance hall until the caller came out, a few minutes later. He was a middle-aged man, pleasant but worried-looking. What an unhappy situation! So this was why the staff was small, the infirmary sparsely furnished! Cherry allowed a few moments to pass for Mrs. Harrison to compose herself, then rapped on the doorframe.

"Come in, Cherry! Don't look so embarrassed. Most of my staff knows about this situation. Everybody is being wonderfully helpful—"

What Mrs. Harrison wanted of her was to ask that the utmost economies be practiced in the infirmary—without, of course, sacrificing high quality of health care. Cherry agreed wholeheartedly. She would have rolled up her sleeves and washed dishes and cleaned house if this lovely woman had asked it of her.

Cherry was careful not to repeat what she had overheard, but she did give Lisette a hint. Perhaps knowing at what sacrifice her scholarship had been awarded, Lisette might concentrate more on her studies and good relations with the other girls.

"I already suspected what you're telling me about the school's financial troubles," Lisette said. She was helping Cherry turn and air the mattresses of the infirmary beds, before the day's classes began. "I could tell you a lot more guesses I've made."

"Well, don't! I have no right to know, though I want to help. How come you guess so much?"

"Oh, well. Like the time Mrs. Harrison told me she couldn't afford a full-time gardener." Lisette looked quietly at Cherry for a moment, then changed the subject. "Have you stumbled across anything? Any clue of the doll?"

Cherry shook her head. "Have you?"

"Nothing yet," Lisette answered.

They agreed it was going to be a big job to search the whole house. They decided to plan this search systematically.

"Mrs. Harrison wouldn't like us to search, either," Cherry said slowly. "It might upset her, and she's worried enough already."

"But, Cherry, it's so important to try this thing! I waited three years for this chance, ever since I found the journal in my father's trunk. We're not trying to deceive Mrs. Harrison, goodness knows. She trusts us; she trusts all her girls. Who'd want to deceive such a darling?"

"Yes, the girls respond well," Cherry said. "There are a few exceptions, like Sibyl—"

"Couldn't we just *not* tell her? Not yet? Until we actually find something?"

Cherry uneasily agreed to that. It was not the most desirable way to handle this unusual situation, but it was the most considerate of Mrs. Harrison. Lisette noticed that Cherry had misgivings, and said:

"We're not hurting Mrs. Harrison, and if we're lucky, something pretty fortunate could come out of it. It could be a real help to Mrs. Harrison, too. It's on her property, so she deserves to share in it financially. Not that she'd believe me *now*. And I don't want to raise her hopes.

"Cherry," Lisette continued, "it's wonderful that you're going to help me. You know a lot about—things a nurse is trained in, and we're going to need technical knowledge." She smiled anxiously at Cherry.

"Don't worry. We'll figure out a plan of search this evening."

In the corridor the bell rang, announcing it was five minutes before the first class. Lisette gathered up her books and hockey tunic, and moved toward the door. She hesitated.

"Tell you what I *am* worried about. It's *l'affaire* bracelet. Sibyl Martin hasn't come back yet, and I don't know which is making me more jittery—imagining what's going to happen or actually facing it."

"You *are* a worrier. Sibyl can't eat you alive."

"That's what you think! She'll be back before this week is out." The last warning bell rang. "Excuse me, now," and Lisette left at a run.

Cherry, too, was impatient to settle once and for all the matter of the lapis lazuli bracelet.

On Thursday the plan was ready, and she and Lisette managed to spend the evening together. Almost all the rest of the school went off by bus to a Gilbert and Sullivan production in Riverton. Lisette had pleaded, in all honesty, that Gilbert and Sullivan put her to sleep, and could she be excused from going? Now the two friends had the house practically to themselves and were able to search in earnest for the doll.

They had done much debating about where to start searching, after all these years. Lisette did not know whether it was a big doll or a tiny one; a breakable bisque doll or a rag doll; that could be a factor in where it lay hidden. However, they agreed there was no point in looking on kitchen or library shelves, since nothing could remain hidden for long in these much-used rooms, nor in the remodeled, newly furnished rooms. This meant the girls would concentrate on the downstairs sitting room and dining room, which had not been remodeled, and upstairs on the infirmary and faculty sitting room which were still big, old-fashioned rooms. Further, Cherry and Lisette had decided that they would examine first the older pieces of furniture which dated from the great-grandfather's day.

The dining room, though furnished with antiques, yielded nothing of interest. They would try the sitting room next, and its old rosewood furniture.

"Still," Lisette said, as they stood on the threshold, "before this house was opened as a school, and that was before Mrs. Harrison took it over, some of the original pieces of furniture must have been removed. And all the closets and cabinets must have been cleared out."

"So we may never find the doll. Try to think," Cherry urged. "Doesn't the journal give any hint where he hid the doll?"

"No, none."

It took boldness to slip into the sitting room and search, with a light showing under the sliding doors from the headmistress's office. They'd thought Mrs. Harrison had gone to the theater. As they tiptoed upstairs, they saw her golden head bent over her desk.

The upstairs was not, as Lisette said, the most encouraging place to search because of extensive remodeling. She believed, from chats with Mrs. Harrison, that the infirmary and faculty sitting room were pretty much as they had been originally, with only minor changes. They decided to try the infirmary first. The oldest piece of furniture in there was probably the extra chest.

"Would the doll be sleeping all these years in the old fruit-wood chest?" Cherry wondered aloud.

The worn, roomy chest stood in the infirmary to provide extra drawer space, but Cherry had never needed to use it except once. She had stored in its top drawer some new linens which Mrs. Harrison had ordered earlier, and which she kept in reserve. Having found nothing in the top drawer or in the drawer beneath, and not needing extra drawer space, Cherry had seen no reason to go through all the many drawers of the chest.

But now she and Lisette did so. They found nothing. The bottom drawer stuck. Lisette burst out laughing at Cherry's struggle with the balky drawer. It was wedged so tight that Cherry teetered back on her heels. "This drawer is trying to knock me down!"

Both girls bent and pulled and got the bottom drawer open. They found only a bundle of old rags wedged in there.

"Anyway, I hope the drawer won't stick any more," Cherry said. It stuck a little just the same, and they laughed.

They tried to be quiet in the infirmary, moving around directly above the headmistress's office. The infirmary yielded nothing. Cherry's room yielded neither doll nor clue. With their hearts in their mouths—"though I have a right to be in here," said Cherry—they hastily searched the faculty sitting room. Nothing to be found there, either. This evening they exhausted their careful plan—without result. They were disheartened.

"Are you certain there *is* a doll?" Cherry asked.

"The journal says so. I'll show it to you tomorrow. Maybe if you look at the journal, you'll notice a clue I missed. Listen!"

They both listened. The chartered bus with its load of girls and instructors was rumbling into the driveway.

"I'm supposed to be in bed by now!" Lisette exclaimed. "Good night!"

Next morning Cherry started to throw away the bundle of rags. She noticed an edge of faded, flower-sprigged dimity—a scrap from an old dress?—and out of curiosity unrolled the cloths. She felt a hard core inside the bundle. Unrolling faster, Cherry's fingers began to make out the shape of it. With the last wrapping removed, she found herself holding a doll which stared at her with painted eyes. If she hadn't noticed the dimity—!

It was a charming little figure, about eight or nine inches high. Judging by its jointed wooden body, its painted head and hands and high button shoes, it must be quite old. The doll wore a long, draped Victorian dress of plum silk, and her black painted hair was demurely parted in the middle. She carried a deep reticule or handbag, its ribbon drawstring tied to her wooden wrist.

"I must show her to Lisette right away! Or at lunch hour, at least tell her what I've found!"

Lisette had a full day's lessons, and Cherry did a full day's work, before they were able to meet in the early evening. Lisette came dashing into the infirmary hugging a flat tissue-papered parcel under her arm.

"Let's see it, Cherry! I'm ready to burst! Oh, where is *la poupée?*"

Cherry ran to the balky drawer where the doll had lived for so many years. "Close the door, Lisette. Here's your doll!"

"Not mine, my great-grandfather's—or rather, his sister's. She brought it from France. Great-grandfather kept it after his sister died. Isn't she a funny, stiff little thing?"

"Has she a name?" Cherry asked.

"The journal doesn't refer to the doll by name, but it does say something intriguing about her. Look!"

Lisette removed the tissue paper and put the old diary

in Cherry's hands. Cherry understood that now Lisette trusted her fully. Its brown leather covers were crumbling at the edges. Within were pages filled with spidery Spencerian script in faded ink, written in French.

"You'll have to translate, Lisette."

"I can do it. Did you know I studied hard by myself to master French—we didn't speak *that* much French at home—so that I'd be able to read this old journal?" She leafed through, looking for passages concerning the doll. "Here it is—

*"The best I can do under these unhappy circumstances is to cache my secret and rely upon the doll to unlock my story, if that day ever comes."*

The two girls stared at each other. It was as if a voice three generations back had spoken, a voice sad or troubled, but urgent. Why were the words veiled?

"Whatever does he mean?" Cherry asked. "You've read the entire journal, I imagine."

"I only know that great-grandfather Pierre Gauthier left behind a valuable and lovely secret in this house. The whole journal is written in this cautious way. You and I will have to sort of decipher it."

They reread the doll passage. *"Cache my secret"*—they debated that. To cache meant to hide something, a tangible thing, but was that what the phrase *said?* Lisette insisted she was translating the words literally and this was not an idiom which had a second meaning. Unable to understand the first phrase, they went on to *"rely upon the doll to unlock my story."*

"Unlock," Cherry mused. "A key? Does the doll contain a key?"

Their fingers shook as they tried to unscrew its head—but this was nailed and jointed on. Next, they felt the folds of its voluminous dress, and looked inside its reticule.

"It's here! It's in here!"

Lisette extracted a narrow key with a filigree handle.

Someone knocked at the door. The two girls jumped. "Just a minute," Cherry called.

Quickly they put the doll, key, and journal into the bottom drawer. The drawer would not close entirely, so they stuffed a towel on top.

"Coming!" Cherry called, and whispered to Lisette, "Throw away that tissue paper, too."

Then she went to the door, slightly out of breath, and opened it. There stood Dr. Alan Wilcox. He looked as firmly planted as an oak tree.

"Thought you weren't going to let me in. We came to pay a more or less social call." He nodded hello to Lisette.

"Who's we?"

"My father, Leaping Lena, and I. Leaping Lena is my car. Can you come out for a drive? We can guarantee moon, stars, and Jamestown's finest ice-cream cone."

Cherry knew that it was out of the question—not with the records that needed to be filled out and special diets to be made up.

She accompanied Dr. Alan downstairs to meet his father. The senior Dr. Wilcox was a quiet, graying man. He asked businesslike questions of the nurse. His smile, like his son's, was full of humor and kindness.

"I hope I didn't detain you, sir," said Cherry.

"Not at all, Miss Cherry."

Dr. Alan said in his most formal professional manner, "You girls were so slow in opening the door, I thought you must be digging for buried treasure, or something."

"You never can tell." Cherry chuckled. "Will you come and dig with us, Dr. Alan?"

He thought she was joking, but great-grandfather Pierre Gauthier was not the only one who was obliged to speak in riddles.

## CHAPTER VI

# *Sibyl*

THE DAY SIBYL MARTIN RETURNED TO THE SCHOOL, excitement broke out—so much excitement that Cherry came down to the stair landing. Sibyl swept into the entrance hall, with the chauffeur carrying in her suitcases and hatboxes and a huge bouquet of early chrysanthemums.

"For Mrs. Harrison," she said sweetly. "Peace offering. Jan! All you infants! Was I ever glad to get away from here! What a time I had at Sis's wedding—my dress was *gorgeous*. I brought it to show you. Going to wear it for when—you know."

"Did you catch the bride's bouquet, Sib?"

"Were there a lot of showers and parties first?"

"I'll bet you saw Freddie somewhere, too, didn't you? Come on, admit it."

Sibyl pouted and posed and smiled over her shoulder meaningfully at Lisette. A group of the younger girls were just coming in from classes in the other building and stood transfixed by this brilliant figure with the red-gold hair.

"Nobody'd think you're only sixteen, Sibyl," Fran said. "Those chi-chi shoes! Those eyes! That hair!"

"I'd say she was sixteen," Mrs. Harrison said, coming out into the hall. "Welcome back, Sibyl. Where did you get those mums? How fresh and lovely they are—and oh, those gay slippers. Can you really walk in them?"

"Why, certainly." Sibyl hobbled shakily on the extremely high heels.

"I remember it takes practice," Mrs. Harrison observed with a twinkle. Some of the girls looked amused. Some of the crowd melted away. The rest trooped after Sibyl as if she were the Pied Piper. She was saying loudly, "I missed wearing my lapis lazuli bracelet, though—"

Lisette came up to Cherry on the stairs and said in a low voice: "She *likes* to torment me. How soon are you going to give her back her wretched bracelet? I'll do it if you don't want to bother."

"No, I'll do it, because I have something to say to her. Don't look so cross, Lisette. Maybe Sibyl isn't as horrid as you think. She's young and foolish."

"Aren't we all? Including you, I'll bet. I will *not* give that meanie the benefit of the doubt."

And Lisette rushed off, her ivory face even paler than usual and her eyes burning like coals.

Cherry had no intention of prolonging Lisette's discomfort. She left a note under Sibyl's door requesting her to stop by the infirmary that same evening.

Sibyl took her time about coming in. Probably, Cherry thought as the evening wore on, she was holding court and recounting her triumphs to practically the assembled school. There was no doubt about it, Sibyl had a way of creating excitement. "Sibyl's the kind of girl things happen to!" the other girls said enviously. "Only," Cherry thought, "what *sort* of things?" She wished she could make Sibyl realize that although it might be exciting to jump off a roof, it would also mean risking a broken neck.

At nearly ten Sibyl came in. In the white infirmary, the bright colors of her dress and hair were intensified. She dropped into the nurse's chair.

"I suppose I've missed a shot or pill or something, Miss Ames." She put on her sweet guileless expression for this official contact.

Cherry said she only needed a little information to complete Sibyl's records, and then chatted with her about what fun weddings are, and the Gilbert and Sullivan they had both missed, but the conversation dragged, so Cherry gave up and came to the point.

"I have something to show you, Sibyl." The bracelet was in the pocket of her uniform.

"To show *me*?" Sibyl sounded bored.

"Yes. Here. Isn't this yours?"

Sibyl started out of her chair. "Why, yes! Yes, of course it's mine!" She reached for the bracelet but Cherry did not give it to her. "May I ask where you found it, Miss Ames? Or perhaps Lisette returned it to you."

Cherry lost her temper. "Stop accusing innocent people! Lisette had nothing to do with your bracelet! But your friend Freddie did."

"Wha-a-at?" She lifted her chin. "That's the silliest thing I ever heard. Freddie is a dear friend of mine." Sibyl turned haughty, hand outstretched. "I'll trouble you for my bracelet, Miss Ames."

Cherry handed it to her without comment. Sibyl looked the bracelet over and put it on. She glanced at Cherry, but the silence continued. Sibyl wriggled in discomfort.

"I didn't mean to sound rude just now, Miss Cherry. I was certain as anything I had left it on my dressing table, but I did wear it on that date. I guess you meant Freddie found my bracelet in his car, didn't you? It must have come unclasped and fallen on the car floor." Sibyl arched her wrist, making the pendant stones swing back and forth. "So Freddie returned the bracelet through you. That was cute of him."

"I'm afraid it wasn't that way." No use mincing words. "I found your bracelet for sale in an antique jewelry shop in Riverton. A young man had brought it in a few days after your date. He told the shopkeeper

*"May I ask where you found it, Miss Ames?"*

it would help pay for his next date at the Golden Door Inn."

Sibyl was so stunned that her mouth fell open. She was unable to say a single word. Cherry felt sorry for her.

"Oh, Sibyl, don't you see? That's how your gallant Freddie can afford to take you to swank restaurants—by selling your bracelet."

"He isn't a bad character, though," Sibyl defended him. "Even if he—"

"He's weak at least, and that's bad enough. I want you to promise that you won't date Freddie secretly again," Cherry urged.

Sibyl's lips trembled. She took a deep breath. "Pooh! I had some more gorgeous dates with Freddie just last week, and I don't care what you think or about silly school rules, either. And I'm going to go right on dating him. Now don't be angry, Miss Cherry. At least I'm not lying to you."

"Doesn't the fact that Freddie found and then sold your bracelet indicate—"

Sibyl jumped to her feet. "Freddie wouldn't do such a thing! Someone else found it. The garage man found it, probably, and *he* sold it."

Cherry sighed and stood up, too. Since she could do nothing with Sibyl, she decided to approach Freddie himself. If that didn't accomplish anything, she would report the matter to Mrs. Harrison.

"Well, maybe Freddie is every bit as gallant as you

say. I'd be glad to be proved wrong. Will I see you both at high tea this Friday?" The school was holding open house for visitors from six to nine. "Auntie Collier promises we'll have mountains of turkey sandwiches."

"I suppose Freddie and I will have to put in an appearance. I could wear my black. Freddie *is* cute, Miss Cherry. When you meet him, you'll know he wouldn't do such a thing as sell my bracelet. I—I— Maybe I ought to tell everybody I found it in the closet or something. So the girls will know Lisette didn't take it."

"That's a nice idea."

They parted better friends, yet Cherry felt uneasy. She had been unable to win Sibyl's complete trust. Perhaps she would have better luck with Freddie.

Lisette was immensely relieved that the bracelet affair was settled. She declared to Cherry, though, that she would never like lapis lazuli as long as she lived.

"Now can't we talk about something interesting? Are the *things* safe in the drawer?"

The doll, the key, and the journal were in the drawer, but unfortunately they had to remain there. Work on the search was held up. The infirmary was a busy place, for the first week of October brought three head colds, two cases of hay fever, and one violent case of homesickness. As for Lisette, she was cramming for the first of the monthly quizzes, coming soon.

By Friday, everybody felt fine again and the tea came as a reward after a vigorous week. Open fires, lighted candles, and fragrant bouquets of late garden flowers—

Lisette mourned such prodigal cutting—decorated the downstairs rooms which were all thrown open for the guests. Quite a few mothers, fathers, and brothers had arrived—they would stay overnight in the village and be here Saturday, too. Also present were a group of boys from the neighboring "brother" school. Most of the boys were shy and stayed together, but a few floated around with nonchalant ease. One of these young sophisticates was Freddie Barnes.

He was attractive looking, Cherry admitted to herself, and about as spoiled as Sibyl. Sibyl, in her grown-up black dress and pearls, looked a sleek twenty years old. She shadowed Freddie, who was busy charming people right and left.

Cherry lost sight of them when dancing started in the dining room. The tables were gone, the floor was waxed to mirror shininess, and a three-piece dance orchestra from St. Louis struck up a tantalizing beat. Cherry wished Dr. Alan could have come. She danced with three girls' brothers, with Mr. North and Mr. Phelps, and felt like somebody's maiden aunt, aged ninety. Turkey sandwiches consoled her, and still more comforting was the sight of Lisette enjoying herself in the gay commotion of a young group.

Then Cherry saw Freddie and Sibyl slip out to the side porch. She saw them whispering and she was worried. Presently Sibyl came back into the house wearing a secretive expression. That meant Freddie might be alone or easily pried loose from the other boys of his school. Cherry saw her chance to talk with him and hurried down the side porch after him.

In the hazy evening light he turned as Cherry called: "Mr. Barnes!"

He had no idea who the saucy-looking girl in red was, with her sparkling coloring and dark curls. Freddie Barnes awarded her a knock-'em-dead smile. His expression flattened out when Cherry explained she was the school nurse and wanted his advice about their friend Sibyl.

"*You* want *my* advice?" Freddie said warily. "What's the angle?"

"No angle. Sibyl is asking for trouble. The headmistress doesn't know yet. I'm the only one who knows about her secret dates with you."

"Don't blame me." Freddie jingled the change in his pocket. "I don't force Sib to go out with me, you know. She loves every minute of it."

"It would be better for her if you'd stop inviting her."

"Say, look! I show Sib a slick time. How many girls in this school d'you think ever get their noses inside the Golden Door Inn?"

"And how many couldn't care less? It wasn't nice of you to get money for your expenses by selling her bracelet."

Freddie laughed. "What of it? It's a good joke. Sib isn't mad, so why should you or anybody care?"

"Because you're imposing on her, and she's a pupil here, and we care about what happens to her."

"You mean, you're asking *me* to obey the rules of a girls' school because old Sib's just another schoolgirl, hey? Maybe I'd better find a girl a little older. Now if you'll excuse me, some of the fellows are waiting for me."

"Better think over what you're doing. I'd so much rather *not* go to the headmistress about this."

"I won't promise you a thing," Freddie said sulkily. He stalked off to a parked jeep.

Well, she had tried. Whether Freddie had really paid any heed to what she had said was a big question. She only wished Sibyl would get some sense and acquire a better taste in boys.

When examination day arrived, Nancy Davenport turned up in the infirmary, sick, just as Mrs. Harrison had predicted she would and generally did. Too sick to take examinations, Nancy moaned.

To Cherry's trained eyes the girl was not faking sickness; she *was* sick. Cherry had seldom seen a more wretched specimen. Nancy sagged and ran a slight temperature; her hair hung limp and dull. She complained of headache and being sick at her stomach. Cherry put her into an infirmary bed and did not say one word about the tests.

"Miss Cherry, did you ever feel like you'd swallowed two dozen spoiled eggs and then stood on your head? That's how I feel."

Cherry remembered nausea is also a symptom of appendicitis.

"Well, your complexion has a delicate green tinge. I've telephoned Dr. Alan to come over and admire it."

Nancy tried to brighten but merely hiccuped.

"He's so nice, I don't want him to see me when I'm the color of pea soup. Ugh, why did I mention that? How soon will he be here?"

Dr. Alan arrived as the bell rang to announce the second class hour, and the second quiz. These were only fifteen-minute quizzes, both the doctor and nurse knew, just monthly brushups, and no reason for Nancy to go into one of her declines.

"If we weren't on dry land," Dr. Alan declared, after checking Nancy over with Cherry's assistance, "I'd say you were seasick. Seriously, my diagnosis is an attack of worry, and a probably self-induced upset stomach."

"That's a horrid, unfair diagnosis," Nancy protested. "I wish you felt as awful as I do."

"No, thanks!" Dr. Alan said. "Don't try to fool a doctor and nurse. Isn't it a coincidence that last term, and now this term, you managed to get sick at exam time?"

"Honestly, I don't do it deliberately. It's just that, with exams coming, I get so scared I'm sick."

"And then you escape taking your exams, and Mrs. Harrison isn't very strict about make-up exams." Dr. Alan looked across the top of their bedraggled patient's head to Cherry. "Miss Cherry, as the nurse in this case you will administer bismuth paste, and a diet of plain boiled rice. We'll cure this girl."

He did not say of what. Alan wrote out his instructions and strode out before Cherry had a chance to gesture that in her humble opinion he was judging Nancy pretty severely. She hurried after him in the hall, but he grinned, waved, and ran down the staircase two steps at a time.

Cherry went back to the infirmary and gave her patient a glass of warm salt water. This was a simple method to empty Nancy's stomach. Nancy obligingly threw up, then said she felt worse. "You'll feel better now," Cherry promised, and lowered the blinds, placed a screen partly around Nancy's bed for privacy, and urged her to sleep. When the girl dozed, Cherry called in Mrs. Snyder, the housekeeper, to sit there a few minutes. Cherry went downstairs to the kitchen.

"Good morning, Auntie Collier. Could you tell me something I need to know, please? Has Nancy Davenport been eating anything beside her regular meals, that you know of?"

"That child! Is she sick to her stomach? It's small wonder. Now, mind you, Miss Cherry, I didn't *give* her all those biscuits. She begs and coaxes 'em from me, at all hours, till I break down and let her have 'em, just to get the child out from underfoot."

The biscuits, it developed, were leftover and hard.

Auntie Collier reported that Nancy had behaved in this manner about once a month last year.

"She craved biscuits a few days before exams?" Cherry asked.

"Yes'm, I think so. I *tell* her not to eat them, I tell her to let me soak 'em in water and toss 'em on the grass for the birds. But that Nancy, she spreads peanut butter all over 'em and—"

"And I can guess the rest. Thanks, Mrs. Collier."

Cherry made a stop at Nancy's room for her bathrobe. Her roommate, shy little Mary Gray, was in there, cleaning up for luncheon.

"How are you, Miss Cherry? I spilled paint all over my shoes in arts and crafts this morning, so I—" Mary gulped in embarrassment and held out the shoes.

"Pink and green dappled shoes. Hmm, you might start a new style. Can you find Nancy's bathrobe for me?"

Mary went to one of the two closets, giving the nurse a look half guilty, half puzzled. "I knew Nancy wasn't feeling right but—ah— Nothing."

"Are you trying to tell me something?" There was a loyal silence. "Can you tell me what Nancy has been gorging herself with?" Mary blushed. "Well, can you give me Nancy's bathrobe?"

Mary opened the closet and out tumbled several candy-bar boxes, mostly empty. A peanut-marshmallow-caramel-chocolate-coated conglomeration appeared to be Nancy's favorite. Its name was *Wow* and Cherry remarked it should be *Ow*.

"She bought 'em wholesale," Mary said sadly.

"When?"

"Well, maybe I shouldn't tell you this—it's one of those intimate things between roommates. Well, Nancy got the candy bars a week ago. She said she'd eat them while we crammed for the tests, because she needed extra strength."

"Do you mean to say that she consumed four boxes? Singlehanded? What about you, Mary?"

"I stick to hard candy," Mary said conservatively.

Cherry took the bathrobe and returned to her patient. Nancy had made herself ill, if not consciously, then accidentally on purpose. Anybody with a grain of sense would know that even anyone with a cast-iron stomach could not digest four dozen *Wows* plus leftover biscuits.

Was it, though, a matter for punishment? The gorging looked on the surface like a deliberate plan. Yet it was a known medical fact that some people, when worried or frustrated, stuffed themselves with food. The real question here, Cherry thought, was *why* did Nancy take this elaborate route to dodge her exams. She was an average bright girl, and her roommate testified that Nancy had been studying. Why were exams such a crisis for her? Other girls had stage fright before exams, but not to this extreme.

The day wore on. The only visitors to the infirmary were Mrs. Harrison and two sufferers with postquiz headaches. Cherry concentrated on Nancy. To allow her digestive system a rest, Cherry gave Nancy for lunch and supper only the plain boiled rice which Dr. Alan had prescribed. She did not let her have water, either, but gave cracked ice to relieve her thirst.

By evening, after a back rub, Nancy felt much better. Cherry judged she was well enough to talk.

"How could you be such a goop?" Cherry asked, point-blank. If she said *foolish* Nancy might be on guard, but the word *goop* was comfortably vague and friendly.

"Was I a goop? Yes, I was. I don't know why."

"Well, think why."

"Because I was so hungry. I felt worn to a frazzle when I was getting ready for exams."

Cherry did not doubt that. "But why so tired at the mere prospect of exams? If you were tired *after* exams, that would be more understandable. Nancy, tell me something. What would happen to you if you failed the exams?"

Nancy groaned. "Don't mention such a horrible subject. It's all too likely."

"Likely? Then you expect to fail?"

"Well, I—not exactly—although—"

"You're so afraid of failing that you'd rather not risk taking exams?" Cherry persisted. "Is that it?"

Evidently she had touched a tender spot. Nancy twisted the ends of her hair around one finger, and gazed at the ceiling.

"Now listen to me, Nancy," Cherry said sympathetically. "Almost everybody is scared of something, whether it's mice or lightning or exams. Sometimes there's sufficient reason for being afraid—sometimes there isn't. It helps to figure out what would result if, just *if,* you happened to fail the exams."

Cherry waited. Nancy lay thinking. Her face clouded.

"My parents would be furious with me. They'd be so terribly disappointed. They're always saying, 'We want to be proud of our daughter.' And what brilliant students they both were in college! And you know how the girls here laugh about anyone who can't make the grade. They'd act as if I was a feeble-minded dodo."

"Discouraging," Cherry admitted, "but look here! Have you ever actually failed an exam?"

Nancy made an effort to remember. "No, I don't think I ever failed one. But that doesn't prove I won't."

"What were your average marks last year?"

"Between eighty and eighty-five."

"Why, that's very good! Especially for a goop, so-called. Do you do good work in class when there are no quizzes to unnerve you?" The girl nodded. "Nancy, it looks to me as if your fear of exams is unnecessary, exaggerated out of all proportion to the facts. You've blown up a fantasy as one blows up a balloon. Let's stick a pin in it."

Cherry's idea (depending on the headmistress's approval) was that Nancy was to take all exams, and, if she failed, no one but the instructor and Nancy would know. Then the other girls could not tease her, and her parents could not be disappointed or furious.

Nancy was uneasy about trying this system. She looked almost sick again when Cherry insisted she start with taking the quizzes missed today.

"And if you should fail," Cherry said gently, "we can ask Mrs. Harrison not to schedule make-up exams until you've had a period of study."

"Miss Cherry, maybe you're going to be my ruination, as Auntie Collier says about the biscuits. But I certainly do thank you for opening my eyes, or at least trying to. I think I see a tiny bit of what you mean already."

Next day Nancy was cured. Next day, too, Mrs. Harrison agreed with her usual kindness to the plan Cherry suggested. A couple of days later Cherry heard that Nancy had taken make-ups on all the missed quizzes. The instructors probably had her papers graded by now. Cherry did not ask how Nancy made out. Then she saw Nancy bouncing around in the corridor, handing out her remaining candy bars to the other girls and shouting, "Get 'em while they're hot! Dee-licious! Step right up!" Cherry grinned and helped herself.

She knew even before Nancy told her that the girl had passed with flying colors.

A little after nine on Sunday evening, Sibyl Martin limped into the infirmary. Cherry was powdering her nose for her first date with Dr. Alan Wilcox. She was so annoyed and disappointed by this interruption that she had to remind herself a nurse is always on call in an emergency. Sibyl's twisted, swollen ankle was an emergency, all right. The fact that Sibyl was all dressed up in hat, coat, and gloves puzzled Cherry.

"Never mind, Mrs. Snyder. Thanks, anyway," Cherry said. The housekeeper was all settled to pinch-hit for her for two hours. "I'm not going out, after all."

Left alone with Sibyl, Cherry questioned her on how she sprained her ankle. Sibyl kept insisting she had fallen in her room.

In ten minutes Dr. Alan arrived. Cherry asked him to examine Sibyl's ankle and murmured how sorry she was about not keeping their date.

"You're not half as sorry as I am!" Alan said as Cherry walked out to the hall with him.

"Miss Cherry!" Sibyl called. "It's killing me!"

"Do you know what I'd like to prescribe for that spoiled infant?"

"Dr. Alan, we'll have the ice-cream cones yet. That's a promise."

"A good spanking is what I'd recommend for her. I don't believe her account of how she twisted her ankle."

Neither did Cherry but she intended to find out. As Alan went down the stairs, she returned to the infirmary. Cherry cautioned herself not to "take out" her disappointment on the patient. Sibyl had not ruined her evening on purpose.

"Where were you going in all your finery?" Cherry asked. "After the curfew bell, too!"

"Please don't scold me, Miss Cherry. I've had all I can stand for one evening." Her face puckered as if she were about to cry. "Some people are plain cruel!"

Cherry made no reply except to say she thought Sibyl would be better off in her own room tonight than in an infirmary bed. "I'll help you to your room. You can rest your weight on my shoulder, and hobble."

They managed it, with plaintive grunts from Sibyl. Several girls along the hall opened their doors a crack, to peek. Cherry opened Sibyl's door, reached in, and turned on the lights. She saw a "rope," improvised of sheets knotted together. One end of it was tied to the bedframe and the other end hung out the open window.

"Sibyl Martin! What did you think you were doing?" Cherry exclaimed. "Eloping?"

"Ssh! Do you want the entire school to know?" Sibyl sank down on the bed.

Cherry had heard a commotion in Mrs. Harrison's office the evening of the tea—sounds of arguing, and then Sibyl's raised voice. So Mrs. Harrison must have placed Sibyl under strict surveillance and Sibyl's response was to use a sheet ladder to keep a date with someone.

"Was it Freddie?" From the way Sibyl hesitated, Cherry knew it was Freddie and no one else. Cherry looked out the window into the brightly moonlit garden. She saw no sign of Freddie, only a squashed rosebush. Sibyl must have landed in that.

"He was supposed to meet me—with the jeep. We made the date the other afternoon at the school tea." Sibyl started to cry noisily. "And now he didn't—he never even— Oh, Miss Cherry, how can a man be so cruel? Freddie never showed up!"

Cherry held her hand sympathetically. Sibyl wailed: "We were going to be married and all I got was a sprained ankle!"

Apparently—Cherry did some rapid thinking—her words of warning to Freddie, after the tea, had borne results. Perhaps she had not persuaded Freddie of his foolishness; probably she had only made him see Sibyl as a sixteen-year-old schoolgirl, not a sophisticate. But that was enough, as far as results went for the moment. But if they actually had been considering elopement—marriage—they might still go through with it.

"Sibyl," Cherry started gently, "I'm not going to scold you. You've had a bitter experience, this evening. Imagine how many more bitter experiences Freddie would treat you to—if this is the way he behaves at the very beginning!"

Sibyl sniffled and clenched her jaw in a stubborn way. Cherry tried another approach.

"Even if Freddie were the young prince you take him for, don't you think elopement is a rather cheap way to do things? It would be hard on your parents, too. Here they just gave your older sister a beautiful wedding, while you sneak out of school via a bed sheet—"

"That's enough," Sibyl interrupted sharply. She blew her nose. "It *is* cheap. I never thought of it in that light."

"How old is Freddie?"

Sibyl said that he was nearly eighteen.

"You're both too young to get married," Cherry observed. "There probably will be someone in your future you'll like better."

"I can't believe it, Miss Cherry. I'm mad about Freddie."

"Being mad about Freddie isn't enough to base a marriage on. If you marry the wrong person, you can ruin the rest of your life, or at least have an awful, wretched time. I don't think Freddie is worth sacrificing your happiness for, or your parents'. Do you?"

Sibyl sat thinking, chewing a corner of her handkerchief. She burst out, "Freddie never even let me know he wasn't coming!"

"Boys who leave girls waiting at the church, so to speak, don't generally bother to notify them."

Sibyl was incensed. "Freddie didn't drop me! He probably was unavoidably delayed. I wouldn't be a bit surprised if he showed up yet! He was only an hour late when I gave up waiting and dragged myself upstairs to the infirmary."

"Oh, Sibyl, Sibyl! The boys' school is only five or six

miles away and he has a car. At least he could have telephoned."

Sibyl turned a suspicious stare on Cherry.

"Did you just happen to tell him to keep away from me? Or did prissy old Harrison? No one in this stuffy school is going to run my life for me!"

"For heaven's sake, Sibyl, come to your senses," Cherry said wearily, and went out.

Mrs. Harrison would learn the whole story now, if only because of Sibyl's limp. Cherry went down to report to the headmistress, an unpleasant business. A school nurse had to treat a great deal more than upset stomachs and sprained ankles!

CHAPTER VII

# *Surprises*

ONE DAY WHEN THE INFIRMARY WAS QUIET AND EMPTY, Cherry ventured to have another look at the doll and journal. Surely Lisette would not mind.

She eased the balky drawer open and removed the towel she and Lisette had tucked on top. Cherry frowned. She felt around with both hands, then began to dig. The doll and the journal were no longer there!

"How am I ever going to break the news to Lisette? Is there somebody else who suspects the secret in this house?"

She must tell Lisette immediately. The most likely place to find her was—outside of class hours—either in the garden or in the conservatory. Yes, there she was in the conservatory, in a plain blue smock, working with the plants.

"Why, Cherry! I'm honored. Sit down. I'm adding

extra soil, bringing loam in from the garden while the days are still mild. See, I've already transplanted our silvery spray and also I brought more of those three important kinds of roses indoors for the winter."

"Such devotion to flowers! Quite a hobby."

"It's anything but a hobby," Lisette said with uncalled-for intensity. "May I ask why you're looking so glum?"

"I—how am I going to tell you such a terrible thing? The doll and the journal, they're—"

"They're gone."

"You know?"

"Certainly. I took 'em." Lisette tilted her head and laughed. "Poor Cherry, I'm sorry you had a scare."

She explained that with so many people in and out of the infirmary, with sometimes only Mrs. Snyder in charge, she decided her locked overnight case in her closet would be a safer hiding place. She took them in Cherry's absence, and then forgot to tell her.

"We have to have a talk soon," Lisette said. "A long private talk."

"I have time off this evening. We can meet in my room," Cherry offered.

Cherry felt more curious about this coming interview than she was willing to admit.

Right after dinner that evening, Lisette rapped on Cherry's outside door. This door gave entrance from the hall. She slipped in, wearing a bulky gay bathrobe from which she took the journal and the doll. The key was back in the doll's purse again for safekeeping. Lisette also brought a French-English dictionary: *La Petite Larousse.*

"Some passages in Great-grandfather's journal are so cryptic they could mean several things. What do you make of this one, Cherry?"

Lisette opened at once to the right page, as if she knew this old diary almost by heart. First she read the passage aloud in French. Cherry did not comprehend too well, though she recognized the liquid purity of Lisette's accent. Then Lisette read the same passage to Cherry in English:

*"Is one reduced to putting one's trust in a doll? Must a lonely old man, the last of his generation, who in his own house has not a soul to talk to, lock his secrets in his heart? Or will the very walls hold his secret? I have lived so much and experienced so much in these rooms that sometimes I feel the chateau itself must know my dearest ideas. Fantastic? Not at all. One is thus reduced. But I forget it is no longer my own house."*

Cherry was deeply moved. She heard the great-grandfather's appeal without fully understanding the sense of his message.

"Why was it no longer his own house?" Cherry asked.

"We'll come to that in a minute." Lisette was referring to the dictionary. "Look, he used a tricky word. This passage could mean entirely different things depending on how you translate *J'ai experiencé.* That could mean *I have experienced so much in these rooms,* or it could mean *I have tried so much or so hard,* or quite possibly it could mean *I have experimented so much in these rooms.*"

"Quite a difference. What do you think it means? You've read the entire journal and you know the context—"

Lisette closed the journal. "Let me tell you the whole curious story. That is, as far as the diary tells it. It was enough to bring me to this house."

Pierre Gauthier, born in 1865, had come from France to the United States when a very young man. He came with his family, including a little sister whose doll this was. He soon married and built the chateau for his bride. He also planted the garden with its roses and some rare flowers, using seeds and shoots he had brought from France.

Pierre and his wife lived happily here and had a son, Louis, who was Lisette's grandfather. Louis grew to maturity and married, bringing *his* bride to live in the Chateau Larose. They had a son and a daughter. The son was Lisette's father. Pierre was glad of the presence of the younger people at first, because his wife had died and he missed her keenly. To fill his time he continued his business as a grain dealer, and visited his neighbors, especially those who also planted gardens. But as he aged, Pierre could no longer work nor go out every day. His son and daughter-in-law, who were devoted to him, urged him to find a hobby that would

*"What do you make of this passage, Cherry?"*

not tax his strength. This was how he started with his experiments.

"Experiments?" Cherry asked. "In the sense of research?"

"Well, he called it a search, and his son and daughter-in-law called it tinkering."

His family never took his "tinkering" seriously, according to the journal. They considered that the elderly man was tiring himself unduly, and they admitted the heavy scents involved became rather oppressive. Pierre complained to his journal that Louis, his son, laughed a little at "Papa's pet folly"; no one had any real comprehension of what he was trying to achieve.

Cherry broke in, in impatience. "Heavy scents of *what?* Chemicals? Cooking?"

"Not exactly. You've noticed the garden—his garden—and how fragrant and unusual the flowers are? Well, he was making perfume. Or at least trying to, for several years. According to what Great-grandfather wrote in the journal, he believed he came close to creating an exquisite and rare scent. Thought he had it almost perfected."

Only, his son and daughter-in-law did not believe in the seriousness of his efforts. They meant well, but they were concerned about his long hours of work in his bedroom. Their good intentions led to unhappy results, quite accidentally.

One day Pierre had gone out, despite the rain, to obtain a few additional fawn roses from a distant neighbor's garden. That week the chateau was being repainted, plastered, and papered, and Pierre's absence for the day provided a convenient time to work in his room. Both Louis and his wife were at home to oversee the job, but since they had never taken old Pierre's experiment very seriously, they were careless or ignorant in regard to his precious ingredients, bottles, and tools. He had set these up in a niche in the wall which, with shelves built in, served as a medicine cupboard. Louis and his wife thought this old wall cupboard ugly, so they told the workmen to plaster it over, apparently forgetting about the contents. When old Pierre arrived home that evening, with the roses for his final experiments, he found that his precious work had been walled in. All he had left, because he always kept it in his pocket, was the filigree key. But the cupboard with its valuable contents was now lost behind a thick wall of rapidly hardening plaster. The son and daughter-in-law were truly sorry about the accident. The great-grandfather pleaded with them to rip out the new plaster. But they regarded that as an old man's nonsense.

Pierre was old, weak, alone, and thus unable to tear out the plaster himself. Besides, he had deeded the chateau over to the younger people, so that it was no longer his house to do with as he pleased. He was dependent on his son. He tried to resign himself to the loss of his little homemade laboratory, to the stoppage of his experiments. All of this Pierre confided to his journal.

"Poor man! Did he write down parts of the formula, too?" Cherry asked.

"Very little. Great-grandfather's notes are hard to decipher at times, but vague references hint that the formula must be in the walled-up cupboard," Lisette replied. She went on to tell about the other entries in the journal.

For some time the old man had been supposed to make a sea voyage to France. The journal was not clear as to whether this was entirely at his doctor's recommendation to aid his health or whether he had some other reason—perhaps connected with his perfume discovery—for traveling to France. By this time transatlantic travel was popular, and the great liners were booked far in advance. Shortly after the incident of the walled-up cupboard, Pierre received a telegram that the reservation for his steamship passage was now available.

The old man, bewildered by the speed of events, hoping still to reopen the sealed cupboard somehow when he returned, took the best precautions he could. He hastily secreted the key in the doll's purse, and hid the doll. Then he recorded the hiding place in his journal as a reminder to himself, but in cryptic language so that no one else could intrude on his work a second time, and cautiously took this personal journal with him.

"Poor old fellow!" Cherry exclaimed. "So he sailed

to France in a sad frame of mind. How did things go when he returned?"

"He never returned," said Lisette. "He never even reached France. He died during the voyage out. See how the diary breaks off short. The very last words he wrote are—"

Lisette showed Cherry the last page of delicate script, and translated: *"I still hope. So lovely, so joyful a fragrance!"*

"Imagine," Cherry said softly, "for him to put his heart into it like that. If the perfume resembled this garden, it might have been as lovely as he believed. I hope so."

"I'm so glad to hear you say that!" Lisette's white face glowed. "That's exactly how I feel! Just think, everything has been waiting here in this house for two decades or more, exactly as Great-grandfather left it on that rainy day. The doll has been waiting all these years behind the stuck drawer. His formula, and possibly even his ingredients if they were tightly corked, are waiting somewhere in this house—*waiting for us to find them!"*

Cherry could not help smiling at Lisette's excitement. First she suggested they talk more quietly, or the whole inquisitive school would come knocking on Cherry's door. Then, reluctant but practical, Cherry asked Lisette what she hoped to gain by recovering the perfume. Was it to vindicate Pierre and fulfill his long hope? Or did Lisette think, *if* they could find and figure out his formula and *if* they could make up a sample, that his perfume might have some market value?

"Yes, to both reasons!" Lisette exclaimed, then clapped her hands over her mouth. "Ssh. Wouldn't you want to right the wrong done to an innocent person? And if you could, wouldn't you save a lovely perfume from being lost forever? I'm convinced it's good, and I'll bet you the formula could be developed and sold to a perfume manufacturer. Imagine! With that money we could—"

"You're daydreaming." Cherry laughed.

"I'm not! You think I'm a mere dreamer like my father? Please note I actually got to the chateau, I actually studied French, and the chemistry of flower oils and of perfume making—"

"I take it back," Cherry said good-humoredly.

"Well, if the formula is salable, a lovely 'new' perfume would provide a living for my mother and future schooling for me. Also, Cherry, it could give the school some measure of financial help. Not that it would be enough to put the school on its feet financially. But since Mrs. Harrison owns this house, and the formula is in it, she'd be entitled to some compensation."

"Yes, those are all worth-while reasons." Cherry sat thinking for a few minutes. "So this is why you've transplanted the garden flowers—why you've brought them indoors into the conservatory for the coming winter."

"*Certain* flowers. The ones the journal mentions as

being ingredients of the perfume. By distillation, that is—"

"You really have been studying up on perfume making! Where? And when?"

Lisette said she had been fortunate enough last year to attend a high school which gave a thorough elementary course in chemistry. It was a laboratory course, and she had really learned a great deal. Cherry understood, as she had had extension laboratory studies during her nurse's training course.

"But ordinary chemistry doesn't have much to do with perfume scents."

Lisette grinned. "Remember that big library book I've covered with plain paper? Well, its title is *The Preparation of Perfumes*. It's practically a textbook, a technical handbook. Fascinating, too. I've been checking against it the portions of the formula mentioned in the journal."

"You have! Does it sound promising?"

The girl nodded.

"What was the basis or secret of your great-grandfather's perfume?"

"Distinctive flowers. What made it so special, as far as I can tell, was certain flowers whose seeds he brought from France. So far, I'm only guessing which flowers, and of course *some* chemicals are needed, too. But in the journal he named his perfume *Fleurs Blanches et Rouges* or Flowers White and Red, so I thought of white rose, the silvery spray—"

"The fawn rose sometimes is nearly white, or streaked with white."

"Yes, and for red flowers, foremost is the big stunning Provence rose. It originally came from France, where it's used a great deal in making perfume."

"By the way, what's the name of the silver spray?" Cherry inquired.

"I believe it's called silver lace in France. Though, really, the silver spray is more like stalks of lily of the valley or bluebell. We could almost call it silver bells."

The biggest question was one Cherry felt reluctant to ask. In listening to the story, it had become clear to Cherry that the great-grandfather had been interrupted with his perfume before he could either fail or fully succeed. *He* had thought his perfume to be "lovely and joyful," but was that true? How could Lisette *know* this was a delightful fragrance?

In the most tactful words she could find, Cherry hinted at this question. Had Lisette, by some happy chance, ever smelled the perfume? Had some breath of it miraculously clung in the chateau over the years?

"No, I've never smelled it. Even if it hadn't been lost, the perfume wouldn't have a clear-cut scent any longer. But I have faith in Pierre's formula! It's only a blind belief—but you know how haunting the garden smells at night! So that using those flowers most surely, surely would yield a lovely perfume. Of course there's a great difference between the living fragrance of a garden and a bottle of scent—"

Lisette broke off and retired within herself. Cherry reassured her that she was not casting doubts. Although not as convinced as Lisette, still she was willing to give Pierre Gauthier the benefit of the doubt. She was more than willing—eager!—to see what the two of them could rescue from the lost formula.

"First step, of course, is to find the sealed-over cupboard," Cherry thought aloud. "I suppose the key unlocks the wall cupboard?"

"Not sure. Listen to this." Lisette read from the journal: *"The door which protects the cupboard in the wall has been plastered over today* . . . Protects. Does that mean a small door, like the door of a wall niche? Or does it mean a full-sized panel with a knob and all?"

"Let's have another look at the key."

It was elongated and narrow, but that was no indication of what type of door it opened.

"Well, then, Lisette, where is the cupboard located?"

"In a master bedroom, I think. But there were two upstairs, and one downstairs—old houses like this one had huge rooms. One master bedroom might be what is now the infirmary. Or it might be the faculty sitting room."

"Yes, but *where* in these rooms?"

Lisette shrugged. "The diary doesn't say. Remember when I was sick and you found me sounding out the infirmary walls? I was listening for a hollow sound, to find a place that had been plastered over."

"I caught you tapping the library wall, too."

"The library is paneled, and it was his own library. This journal is so awfully cryptic! I s'pose Great-grandfather knew what his own notes meant, even if I don't!" Lisette sighed. "The only way we'll find the cupboard is to tap the walls and listen."

"We may be tapping the chateau all winter," Cherry murmured. "Have you found anything so far?"

"Not a thing. But we will."

CHAPTER VIII

# *Young Dr. Alan*

IT WAS ONE OF THOSE PEACEFUL, SUNNY MORNINGS which Cherry thought was almost too peaceful to be true. Not a single patient to be treated in the infirmary, her records brought up to date, all the equipment shining clean. "For once," she thought, "I could sit and twiddle my thumbs! Not that I want to."

Cherry wished she could explore the house or at least the three largest rooms, which may once have been the master bedrooms, one of which had been Pierre's, to look for his cupboard. It had been on her mind ever since hearing of it evening before last. The fragrance of Lisette's flowers in the sunny conservatory drifted upstairs to her, faint but tantalizing. But a school day, with the staff busy at their tasks all over the house, was not the time to go tapping on walls. Tina or Mrs. Harrison or Mrs. Snyder would think she had lost her mind if they saw her doing such a thing.

The infirmary telephone rang. Cherry reached for it and answered with proper decorum.

"Infirmary, Miss Ames speaking. Good morning."

"Good morning. This is Alan Wilcox. I called to ask whether you could drive to a farm with me and help out on an emergency baby case."

"Well, I haven't a thing to do this morning except a few minor details that can wait. I'll ask Mrs. Har—"

"This call can't wait."

"I'll get my equipment packed right away," Cherry said. Mrs. Harrison would almost certainly grant permission.

"Stop by for you in ten minutes," Dr. Alan said, and hung up.

Cherry moved fast. She reached Mrs. Harrison by telephone and explained the situation. Mrs. Harrison said to go, by all means. She added, "How long has it been since you had a day off, Cherry? With everything under control in the infirmary, I think it would be all right if Mrs. Snyder and I take your place."

"Oh, thank you, Mrs. Harrison!" She heard the headmistress chuckle. "I'll be back before dinnertime, though." Going off with Dr. Alan was important, but her first responsibility was here. She hoped no one at the Jamestown School would break, sprain, bruise, or swallow anything untoward in the next few hours.

In seven minutes flat Cherry packed her nurse's kit

with thermometer, a bottle of antiseptic, paper tissues, sterile cotton, sterile gauze dressings and tape, bandage scissors, forceps, a measuring glass, and hypodermic syringe. She borrowed the infirmary's rubber sheet. She already wore her nurse's watch with sweep-second hand, and slipped her coat on over her white uniform. She dashed downstairs to the entrance porch just as Dr. Alan, hatless in his old convertible, swung up the driveway. He had the car door already open for her.

"Hop in. How long can you stay?"

"As long as you need me."

"Oh, fine. Meet Leaping Lena. Watch her, now!"

On the open road he raced the car up to sixty. He seemed relaxed, but started at once describing the case to Cherry.

"I'm in a jam, otherwise I wouldn't have bothered you. This is a 'premie,' and we may have a bit of trouble. Have you had any maternity-ward experience, Cherry?"

"Certainly. A good deal, Doctor." Did Alan think she was just a youngster?

At the farmhouse they found a distracted young husband awaiting them. It was obvious that, in his anxiety, he would be more hindrance than help, and, as Alan started in to examine the patient, his eyes seemed to give Cherry a message: "First, get this fellow occupied with something so he won't be in the way."

Cherry turned immediately to the young man. She smiled at him reassuringly and said, "I'll need a few things that you can get for me. Please turn on the stove and put a small pan of water on to boil. We'll probably want to sterilize a few instruments. No, not such a big one," she added with a smile, as the boy—he was hardly more than that—produced a huge kettle. "We're not going to boil *you,* you know—just a few instruments."

When a smaller pan was substituted, Cherry said briskly, "Now, since this baby is coming a bit sooner than you expected, it's likely to be small and will need a nice warm nest to sleep in. Get your wife's clothes-basket, and put several soft blankets in it for a bed. I'll be helping the doctor, and all the time we're busy I want you to keep warming the baby's bed with hot-water bottles. Use fruit jars if you don't have rubber ones, and be sure they don't leak. Don't get the blankets too hot, but keep them nice and warm all the time so that you'll be ready the minute we are."

Cherry left him and went in to help Dr. Alan. "It's all fixed," she said. "He'll be busy."

And so he was, for later, when Cherry carried the tiny but perfect baby out for him to see, the basket bed was warm and cozy.

After the young mother was resting comfortably and Dr. Alan had given Cherry her instructions, he turned to the boy and said, "I'll leave Miss Ames here for a bit while I take this young fellow in to the hospital. He's a fine baby and you don't need to worry at all, but he's pretty young to go it alone, and he'll have a better start if he spends the first few hours in an incubator. He'll be back to keep you awake nights in a few days. Now, who's going to take care of things until your wife is able to get along by herself?"

"Her mother was coming, but I couldn't leave Sue," the boy said, "and she doesn't even know yet that we need her. She lives only about ten miles from here, and if Miss Ames is going to stay, I'll go and get her."

So it was arranged, and when Dr. Alan returned he found the new grandmother in competent charge and Cherry ready to leave. He checked his patient and then hustled Cherry into the car, saying, "You've certainly earned a bang-up lunch."

It was late, and they were the only ones being served in the quiet dining room of a country inn. Blazing gold elm branches swung beside the window where they sat.

"Wish it was cool enough for a fire in the fireplace," Alan said, over his second piece of apple pie. "We'll come back here some snowy day and I'll show you how to pop corn over an open fire. This inn always has some on hand."

Cherry started to say she was an expert corn popper from way back, but decided that would spoil Alan's fun. They had talked over the baby case backward and forward, so Alan was entitled to change to a nonmedical subject.

"Wish you could come along regularly as my nurse," Alan said. "We work together very well."

"Thank you."

"It's not exactly a compliment. Just a fact. Just one of

those things. Are you sure you can't hold another piece of this scrumptious pie? I can."

Cherry kept him company, laughing. "If I were your regular nurse, Doctor, I'd soon get fat."

"We're stoking up for an afternoon of hard work, if you can come along. General cases."

"Yes, I can come," Cherry said, "and you couldn't afford to have me as your full-time nurse, anyway. So there," she finished.

"No, I couldn't," he said with regret. "And my father is devoted to Mrs. Kennedy, who's been the local practical nurse since the year one, I guess."

Cherry's dark eyes danced. "I do have an idea that might turn out to be perfect for both of us, Doctor. I call it nursing à la carte."

He looked interested and she explained. In a country or small-town neighborhood, why couldn't an R.N. do hourly nursing, when and where she was needed? Any of the local physicians could call on her services, and of course any of the local patients.

"You'd need a car," Alan said. "To tell you the truth, I've sometimes ordered treatments that an amateur nurse could handle, when a more difficult treatment administered by an R.N. would've been better for the patient."

"Just what I was saying! Still, it's only an idea."

That afternoon was a sample of hourly nursing, mostly assisting the doctor. Dr. Alan and Cherry worked hard on routine calls, and again they worked well together.

"I'll have to buy you that ice-cream cone for a reward, Cherry. Seriously, thanks for everything."

He and Leaping Lena delivered Cherry to the school doorstep late in the afternoon. Alan was going back to the farm to see his patient. They parted reluctantly.

"We're a good team," Alan said. "So long for now."

On the following afternoon a terrible accident happened. Cherry heard the crash and from the infirmary window saw the thin trickle of smoke, smelled spilled gasoline. Everybody in the school heard the crash and went rushing down to the road. In the driveway, teachers were persuading the excited girls not to crowd down there, to turn back. Cherry, with the first-aid kit in her hand and a blanket thrown over her shoulders, kept on running.

A car in which two men had been driving had careened into a tree, buckled, turned over, and caught fire. One man—a young, big man—was thrown free but appeared to be badly injured. Behind the steering wheel was pinned a heavy-set older man, unconscious. Alex North and Mr. Phelps, Perry the houseman, and a passing farmer were already trying to smother the small fire with their coats. They were succeeding. Mlle. Gabriel was looking down at the young man and wringing her hands.

Cherry glanced quickly at both injured men and had to make a hard, instant decision: which one must wait while she treated the other? She knelt beside the young man in the grass. His leg wound, bleeding slightly, looked like a puncture wound and she must prevent infection.

"Mademoiselle!" Cherry handed her a thick gauze pad to use as a pressure dressing and, to use first, a bottle of strong antiseptic. She explained to Mademoiselle what to do. "Saturate the pad and apply it to the wound to close off air bacteria and dirt. Be gentle but be quick. Cover him with this blanket."

Then Cherry ran to help the older man pinned in the car. The fire was no longer a danger but he might have inhaled carbon monoxide fumes and thus have become unconscious. Or the rim of the steering wheel might have struck him in the solar plexus when the car hit the tree; that would mean invisible, dangerous, possibly hopeless, internal injury. Alex North and Sam Phelps were crawling in to move the unconscious man. Cherry cried, "Please wait!"

They helped her clamber into the tipped-up front seat where the man lay, breathing heavily and with difficulty. Cherry hastily checked his pulse and respiration —shallow, irregular breathing—his face was pale and sweaty—was the man suffering from shock or from a heart attack? Considering his advanced years it might be arteriosclerosis. Cherry's hands shook as she fumbled in his jacket pocket, the right-hand pocket first. Yes, there it was! She pulled out the little box of nitroglycerin pills which all cardiacs of this type carry in case of

*Cherry had to make a hard, instant decision*

emergency. Hastily she forced the man's mouth open and placed one of the pills under his tongue, where it would dissolve. She loosened his collar, tie, and belt, and untied his shoelaces. Some color returned to his face and lips, and his eyelids fluttered.

The two men instructors realized what was happening and North said, "Shall we try to get him out into the open air?"

"No. He may have other injuries which we'd make worse by moving him. Can you roll down the car windows to give him more air—and keep him warm with your coats, will you please?"

Cherry knew that someone inside the chateau was surely telephoning the Wilcox physicians and probably the hospital, too. Though a small country hospital with only one ambulance might not be able to send aid at once.

"They're not here but I am—it's up to me!" Cherry thought.

She ran back to Mademoiselle. She and Mrs. Curtis were on their knees in the grass beside the youth, and had applied the dressing. Cherry was thankful that both women were quick and calm. The young man was conscious and in pain. Shock was the greatest danger.

"Keep him warm. Someone bring a warm drink—" Mrs. Curtis started for the house. Cherry considered giving him a half-grain tablet which Dr. Alan had prescribed for Tina, but she had no authority to do so without a doctor's instruction. She leaned over the young man and said encouragingly, "We're going to take you to the school infirmary. The doctor is on his way."

The young man whispered, "You a nurse? That's good."

Five minutes went by. Everybody was eager to help. Some of the girls plucked at Cherry's white sleeve and one whispered in her ear:

"Do you know who the young fellow is? Francie saw him first—we were out with our horses—and she was so excited she nearly—"

"Honestly, don't you know, Miss Cherry? Why, he's Tommy Dexter, and he's *the* football star at State U!"

"Fullback! And the other man is his coach!"

So many girls were fluttering around that Cherry was obliged to admonish them with:

"If you want Tommy Dexter to get well, go away!"

Cherry wished one or the other Dr. Wilcox would get here. She hurried back to the man in the car. Alex North was with him. The older man was breathing normally now, and he was being kept warm. But the husky football star, whom she had worried less about at first, seemed to be going into shock.

His ruddy face was turning pallid, his skin was cold and clammy, his pulse rate rapid and thready. Cherry was concerned that she could feel his pulse only with difficulty. She spoke his name—*"Tom? Tommy!"* but like any person in shock, he did not respond, though he was conscious. Cherry called sharply to Mrs. Snyder to send for more blankets and hot-water bottles. She herself ran to the infirmary, rapidly stirred up a shock solution of warm water, salt, and a little baking soda and ran back with it as fast as she could. She gave the young man sips of this through an angled glass straw—it was safe *only* because he was conscious. She tried to relieve Tommy's pain by very carefully placing a support of blankets beneath his injured leg.

Cherry heard Leaping Lena's familiar engine beat, then the brakes. A minute later Alan and his father were with the two injured men. Cherry was never so glad to see anyone in her life.

"Miss Ames, will you describe what's happened?" Dr. Horton Wilcox demanded.

Cherry stated succinctly and clearly all the facts, and reported Mrs. Harrison's offer of their infirmary as a temporary hospital. Dr. Horton Wilcox went to examine the supposed cardiac case. Dr. Alan gave the younger man an antitetanus shot, Cherry assisting, then removed the antiseptic dressing and injected penicillin into the open wound against possible infection.

Perry was coming from the house bringing a stretcher. Dr. Horton Wilcox requested North and Phelps to help him lift the man from the car onto the stretcher. He was a dead weight. "Keep his head a little lower than his feet. Nurse, keep him covered."

It took Perry and three men instructors to carry the heavy man up the school driveway. Dr. Alan and Cherry accompanied him, at the elder physician's order. Unfortunately the school had but one stretcher, so that a second trip would have to be made for the football star.

In the infirmary Cherry caught sight of Lisette, in a clean smock, scrubbing her hands at the infirmary sink. Good girl! Cherry murmured to her to boil water, which the doctor might want, and to prepare several hot-water bottles. Lisette nodded and went to work. Mrs. Snyder, Mrs. Curtis, and Mademoiselle were waiting here to help, while downstairs Mrs. Harrison had a full-time job preserving order and quiet. Cherry sent all of her helpers out of the room, with Mrs. Snyder on call.

The men having transferred the older man to one of the beds, Cherry removed his shoes and jacket, covered him with a blanket, and on Dr. Alan's order applied hot-water bottles. Then she helped him sip some water and placed a screen around his bed, to shut out distractions. He needed to be entirely quiet. As she worked, she wished she had studied ten times harder at Spencer Nursing School, and vowed she would take some refresher courses soon. She *did* read her professional monthly journals, she *did* study new techniques and practice them. But when lives hung in the balance, depending directly on her skills—

Didn't she hear the wailing of an ambulance siren? It came near and whined to a stop.

Two minutes later Alex North came in, alone and out of breath. He summoned Dr. Alan and the nurse to the infirmary door.

"Dr. Wilcox is taking the boy to the hospital in the ambulance, for a blood transfusion. Shock case, he said.

He's asking you, Dr. Alan, to handle the other patient."

"Thanks, Mr. North. Then my father left the car here?"

"Yes, he did. Dr. Wilcox said to tell you and Miss Cherry that he expects the boy will come out of shock all right. He also mentioned possibly doing emergency surgery, to prevent any chance of a limp later on."

Cherry breathed easier. It seemed to her that she had done very little for Tommy Dexter, but apparently she had done the right and adequate things. Just the same, she'd feel better if Dr. Wilcox had said so. She followed Dr. Alan back toward the occupied bed.

The young doctor proceeded to examine the exhausted man as thoroughly as he could without X rays. He murmured to Cherry that he found nothing which made it necessary to move him at once to the hospital, and that the essential thing was absolute rest for several hours.

Their patient was falling asleep. Dr. Alan moved away from the bed and said to Cherry in a low voice:

"You'll have to stay up all night to watch this patient, Miss Cherry. With a cardiac case, particularly in arteriosclerosis—"

So she had judged right! Dr. Wilcox instructed her in the care of the cardiac during the night. He ordered her, in case of an attack of coronary thrombosis, to summon him instantly and to administer nitroglycerin. "Have you anyone to relieve you? Mrs. Snyder? Good." Alan half smiled at her in encouragement.

"Don't try to turn or lift this patient; he's too heavy for you. If you need help, phone me and I'll come. Let me do any heavy work for you."

All that long night Cherry stayed at her post. The hour before midnight Mrs. Harrison herself relieved her for a nap, and Lisette thoughtfully brought up sandwiches. Cherry put on her thick white sweater and checked TPR, made her patient more comfortable, refilled the hot-water bottles, and sat down beside a dim night light to watch and wait and serve. To keep awake, she wrote letters, rising every fifteen minutes to probe with her flashlight's beam for any sweaty pallor or for any unforeseen development. None, thank goodness. Twice she gave him hot bouillon. By six in the morning she was very tired. But her patient, breathing normally, had come through the night without mishap or even great pain. By breakfast time he was able to smile weakly and say he was hungry.

Dr. Wilcox and Alan arrived at eight to see whether the coach could stand being moved to the hospital. On checking his condition, Dr. Wilcox said he would telephone for the ambulance to come for him at once. Tommy Dexter, they reported, was out of danger and his leg eventually should be as good as ever. This news cheered both Tommy's coach and Cherry.

"Miss Ames, I want a word with you about your nursing service," said Dr. Horton Wilcox. He read again the records she had kept for this night and put them in his pocket.

Cherry trembled. "Yes, Doctor?"

"I admit this was not an easy assignment. All the more reason, then, that you are to be commended. Highly commended. You have obviously had excellent hospital training, and you used it to full advantage in giving first aid, and in the overnight care."

Cherry's knees became weak in her relief. She scarcely heard the rest of what Dr. Wilcox was saying.

"—shall tell Mrs. Harrison so. An exceptionally good nurse! I wish more nurses had your quick wits and common sense."

"Thank you, Dr. Wilcox." But she was looking at Alan, and Alan was smiling at her. Cherry ventured to say: "Well, Dr. Alan, do I still get the ice-cream cone for a reward?"

"A medal would be more like it. You're the best nurse I ever met!"

That was all the reward she could possibly want.

## CHAPTER IX

# *The Disappearing Window*

"SSH! MOVE SOFTLY OR SOMEONE WILL HEAR US!"

Lisette nodded as Cherry noiselessly opened the infirmary door and peered out. The corridor was empty and quiet. It was eleven at night, and everyone was in bed. Lisette and Cherry were presumed to be in bed, too, but this was their first chance, since the emergency of last week, to search for the cupboard niche. According to the journal, though the great-grandfather was maddeningly cryptic, the concealed cupboard was located somewhere in whichever had been his former room. They decided to tap the walls of the infirmary first, as long as they were in there.

"Wish we knew *which* room used to be Pierre's," Lisette fretted. "I tried in a roundabout way to ask Mrs. Harrison"—Cherry fleetingly wondered why Mrs. Harrison should be expected to know such a thing—"because she—ah—saw this house when she was a little girl," Lisette explained. "She said that she didn't exactly remember. It seemed to her that Great-grandfather had occupied different rooms at different times, as his family grew larger or smaller. So that was no help."

"We'll just have to find out on our own," Cherry agreed.

Both girls were padding around softly in slippered feet, with only the night light burning. They wore night clothes, in case any faculty member should suddenly come in, and they also wore warm sweaters. As Cherry remarked, these mid-October nights were chilly, and one loud sneeze would be enough to betray them if the rain and wind should cease.

"Anything over there?"

Lisette was on tiptoe beside the left end of the fireplace, cautiously tapping the wall. "Nothing here. I'll try the whole area, though."

"I'll try the right end of the fireplace," Cherry whispered. She knew medicine cupboards generally used to be built at the left end, but you never could tell.

Both girls tapped, listened with ears against the papered wall, tapped again. They did not hear the hollow sound or faint echo for which they were alert. The whole fireplace wall was solid.

"The cupboard just isn't near the fireplace," Lisette sighed.

"Don't be discouraged. The room is big but not so enormous that we can't cover every inch."

"Where shall we try next?"

"Hmm. With everyone asleep, it's a good chance to try the corridor. The remodeling may have cut off a corner of this room."

With their hearts in their mouths, Cherry and Lisette slipped soundlessly into the hall. Here was a small area of wall between infirmary and faculty sitting room which intrigued Cherry. They tapped it, at eye level, then higher—no point trying lower—when a footstep made them whirl around.

"Hide!" Cherry hissed, and shoved Lisette through the nearest door. It led into the darkened, empty faculty room.

Here came, of all people, Sibyl leaning on the cane which she had used since her fall. She swished along in a negligee, looking sleepy and cross.

"Aren't you feeling well, Sibyl? Can I do something for you?"

"You've already done plenty for me, scaring Freddie away. Oh, I didn't mean that! No, I'm all right, Miss Cherry. What's that funny noise I heard?"

"What noise?"

"Like someone knocking. Moving around, *inside* the walls, maybe. They say these old houses are full of ghosts."

Sibyl shivered, but Cherry grinned.

"Old houses are full of loose floor boards and crumbly plaster. It's windy tonight and the house creaks, that's all. Go back to bed, Sibyl, there's a dear."

"Are you sure that's all?" Sibyl said suspiciously. She pushed her red-gold hair out of her eyes and yawned. "Oh, well, the ghosts can have this wretched old place. *I* don't care."

She limped back to her room and shut her door noisily enough to waken the entire second floor. Cherry held her breath. Two, three minutes went by, but nothing happened. She poked her head inside the faculty room and made out Lisette's dark tumbled hair and pale face.

"Sibyl thinks we're ghosts."

"Well, we're looking for a ghostly kind of thing, aren't we?"

After another half hour of quietly sounding the infirmary walls, Cherry declared under her breath: "I think a ghost would be easier to find than this cupboard. Shall we try another room next?"

Lisette was discouraged, too. She said, "Let's sit down and rest for a few minutes, and try to think." They had been listening for a telltale sound, searching for the cupboard whose keyhole the doll's key might be presumed to fit. So far they had found nothing.

"Wouldn't Mrs. Harrison be astonished if she happened to walk in right now," Cherry mused.

"Don't say such things!" Lisette frowned. "She'd be angry. If she ever learns what we're up to, she'll forbid it."

The girl's vehemence surprised Cherry. "You're awfully positive about what Mrs. Harrison's attitude would be," she said, mildly inquiring. But Lisette shrugged. If she knew something further, she was not telling.

Cherry bypassed the matter, for the time being, and concentrated on where the cupboard might be concealed. Suddenly an idea occurred to her.

"Listen! I just remembered something. Don't know why I forgot about it all this time. Right after I came here, I think the very first evening after supper, when we were in the garden, I happened to look up and noticed a special kind of window."

She described to Lisette the diamond-shaped window of stained glass, with panes of various colors. Since the house had several windows of stained glass here and there, Lisette could not place that particular window.

"As best I can remember," Cherry said, "it should be in the infirmary, on the side wall somewhere between the fireplace and the supply closet."

They glanced at that side of the room. On either side of the fireplace were ordinary plate-glass windows, with blinds. The long, narrow supply closet, placed at a right angle to the fireplace wall, ran about eight feet but had no window. Where was the missing window?

"I could swear I saw that window in about this location," Cherry said.

"Would it be in the faculty room?"

"I'll go see," and Cherry rose, though she did not much like venturing into the corridor where she might be noticed. However, she took her flashlight and went next door to the faculty sitting room.

"No such window in there," she reported back to Lisette.

"And that room is right next to the infirmary," Lisette said. "No hallway in between the two rooms. You know what, Cherry? I think the window may be located farther down."

"There's only one thing to do. That's for me to go down to the garden tomorrow and have another look. Unless— Does the journal say anything about a window?"

Lisette could not recall any reference. She leafed through its faded pages but shook her head.

"Nothing about any window. Wait, though. Here's a passage which has always puzzled me. But it's about— how to translate *la cloison?* Cubbyhole, I guess, or cubicle. Possibly Pierre meant storage space."

"Cubbyhole *where?*" Cherry pricked up her ears.

"Seems to refer to the staircase."

"The big main stairway?"

Lisette nodded.

"But the journal locates the cupboard in a master bedroom. Nowhere near the staircase."

"I told you I didn't understand it, Cherry. Do you suppose he's talking about two separate things?"

"If he is, and the cupboard is one thing, what's the second thing? Anyway, the cupboard is the main object, isn't it?"

They talked round and round the subject, but their reasoning was inconclusive. Talking did not help; what they had to do was search. It had grown too late to hunt any further. The storm was over, and the silence in the sleeping house was profound, so that their tapping would surely reach someone's ears, and Sibyl was already alerted.

Lisette said good night, peered to see if the coast was clear, and fled silently to her room.

Next day it seemed to Cherry forever before she had a few free minutes to visit the garden. The right time came in midafternoon. Her chores were completed, and most of the girls were either out riding or on the hockey field. Cherry figured it was as good a time as any. She slipped downstairs and went out the side door past the conservatory and into the garden.

Standing where she had stood that first day at twilight, she looked up to the remembered spot and saw the diamond-shaped window! So she had *not* been mistaken about its location. It *must* be within or almost within the boundary of the infirmary, because Cherry carefully counted and accounted for all the windows. This window seemed to be an extra one; she noted also that it seemed to be permanently closed, a window for light and decoration only.

There were the two tall plate-glass windows with blinds, which flanked the infirmary fireplace. Next came the diamond-shaped window. Then came the plate-glass windows with chintz draperies, and that particular chintz hung in the faculty room. Therefore the diamond-shaped window might be located somewhere between the infirmary and faculty room. But why hadn't she and Lisette been able to find it?

"I think I have it!" Cherry exclaimed to herself. "I'm not going to waste time speculating, though. Lisette and I will test out my theory this very evening."

On her way back into the house, Cherry looked in at the small conservatory. Now that she understood the flowers were to be used to compound a perfume, she was doubly interested to see what Lisette had transplanted. The young girl had given over most of the conservatory's space to the great-grandfather's delicate, pungent spray called silver lace and to three varieties of roses—Provence, fawn, and China rose. A few other varieties of blossoms thrived here as well.

"I'm lingering too long downstairs," Cherry realized. Yet she could not resist stopping a few more seconds to breathe in the delicious fragrance of the roses and the silver spray.

The happy memory of a recent afternoon returned to her, as she started on her way back upstairs. Dr. Alan had taken her and Lisette for a drive in the beautiful weather, and the two girls had steered the conversation around to local gardens. Because the silver spray was rare, Lisette discussed visiting neighbors' gardens in search of more of this flower. Alan had no idea why the two girls were so interested in flowers and gardens, but, having lived here all his life, he drove them to the minister's garden. There they saw a little silver lace bush. The Reverend Mr. Dixon, Alan had said, was

*Why hadn't she and Lisette been able to find the diamond-shaped window?*

about the only person he knew of who still fancied it and cultivated it. Lisette was all for ringing the doorbell and begging for a promise of some in season, but Alan gave her fair warning. The minister was a man of formidable attainment and, as Dr. Dixon was retired, he did not look kindly on casual visitors. So the three young people had driven past. All of this flashed through Cherry's mind in an instant as she ran up the stairs.

"We'll find some more silver lace somewhere, yet," she thought blithely. "It's only a question of patience and—"

The wide-open infirmary door gave her a jolt. Usually it stood ajar. She hurried in to find Mrs. Harrison standing in the deserted infirmary, extremely annoyed.

"Where have you been, Miss Ames? What are you thinking of, to leave the infirmary unattended and no one notified to relieve you?"

Oh, dear! Mrs. Harrison had called her *Miss Ames* —a bad sign. She could not very well tell the headmistress the inexcusable truth.

"I'm sorry, Mrs. Harrison. I went downstairs for a few minutes."

"For twenty minutes, because I have been waiting here for twenty minutes. Couldn't you have sent someone on your errand? And why is there not an essential remedy like aspirin in this medicine chest?"

Only then did Cherry notice that the medicine chest stood open and that Mrs. Harrison had removed several bottles in her fruitless search for aspirin.

"No aspirin? But I thought—" Cherry searched frantically through the medicine chest and did find the aspirin. Apparently Mrs. Harrison had a bad headache and apparently it had caused her to overlook the right bottle.

"I'm extremely sorry you had to wait, Mrs. Harrison. Here you are," she added, giving her a tablet and a tumbler of water. "Is there anything further I can do for you?"

Mrs. Harrison swallowed the aspirin and said severely, "What you can do for me, Miss Ames, is stay on duty and not go wandering off. I expect you to behave more responsibly than the schoolgirls, you know."

Cherry bit her lip. If only she could tell the headmistress why she had run down to the garden, surely Mrs. Harrison would understand. But Lisette thought not. Well, she was bound by her promise not to tell, and as a result Mrs. Harrison thought the nurse had been negligent.

"Why, oh, why, have I such a talent for getting into trouble with the powers-that-be?" Cherry wondered. She watched Mrs. Harrison's straight, retreating back. "Now that she has an eye on me, more or less, all I need is to be discovered doing some midnight prowling. Then I'll really be in trouble."

She and Lisette would have to be very careful from now on. If they were caught, they both might be sent home. Cherry told the girl so that evening when they met after dinner.

"Perhaps," said Cherry, "we ought to drop our search altogether for a few days. At least until Mrs. Harrison is feeling better and in a good humor again."

"No, Cherry, no! The search *can't* wait. We've got to go right ahead this evening."

"Well, I do have a fresh idea about that diamond-shaped window—"

Cherry waited to tell Lisette in the comparative privacy of the infirmary at nine o'clock. "Lights out" was at ten, so they had only an hour. Cherry had rearranged the medicine chest and put it in apple-pie order earlier in the evening. She felt she had earned the right to spend time now to talk with Lisette.

"About the window—I checked from the garden and you'll be amazed where I suspect it is," Cherry said.

"Don't keep me waiting like this!"

"I think the missing window is *in the supply closet.*"

"Hmm. Frankly, Cherry, I don't understand. Maybe I'm not as quick as you are—anyway, I'm not as old as you are."

Cherry laughed and linked her arm through Lisette's.

"It's simple, my dear Watson. I mean, it's elementary. Follow closely. The journal says, doesn't it, that on the day your great-grandfather was away from the chateau, *some place* in his room was plastered over? Let's assume for the moment that the infirmary was his room, since it's the biggest bedroom in the house. Now, then! You and I have been looking for his medicine cupboard, knowing *it* was plastered over. We've been searching for a small area, but we could be wrong."

"I can't follow you, my dear Sherlock Holmes."

"Listen. Couldn't a whole end of the closet have been plastered over?"

"But why would anyone want to plaster over an inside wall of the closet?" Lisette objected.

"To clean up and modernize, to cover an old, cracked wall. Didn't Pierre's son and daughter-in-law have the plastering and papering done in order to improve the house?"

"Yes," Lisette said. "There's a good chance that during this decorating and modernizing they put a brand-new bathroom in the chateau, with a new medicine cabinet and all."

"So that an old-fashioned cupboard niche in a closet wouldn't be needed any longer," Cherry pointed out.

A light dawned in Lisette's eyes.

"That's right. But how about the window? You think it's at the end of the supply closet, and that end of the closet—"

"—has been sealed off. Plastered over. And I think your great-grandfather's medicine cupboard is—"

"—in the portion of the closet which is sealed off! Cherry, you're terrific!"

"We hope. Let's test it out!"

Both girls rushed to the eight-foot-long closet, went in, and, facing toward the garden, tapped on what was presumably the outside wall of the house. But instead of the solid sound they were used to hearing, back came a hollow echo. Cherry also thought she heard a faint tinkle, like the movement of crumbs of plaster. A false wall—

"That's the place!" Lisette shouted, then held both hands over her mouth.

"It *may* be the place," Cherry said coolly. Her heart was thumping, though. "A simple test is to measure."

She measured the outside wall of the closet: it was eight feet long. She measured the inside wall of the closet: it was seven feet three inches long. Nine inches were unaccounted for, and that was sufficient space to accommodate the door of a wall niche.

But how were they to penetrate to the other side of the plaster barrier? It would mean chiseling or removing that plaster.

"Dr. Alan!" Cherry exclaimed. "He said to let him do any heavy work for me. And removing plaster certainly is heavy work!"

CHAPTER X

# *Inside the Wall*

TO APPROACH ALAN ABOUT GETTING THROUGH THE mask of plaster was no easy undertaking. First, Cherry had to persuade Lisette to share her secret with Alan. For how could they expect Alan to come secretly to the chateau and do something so drastic as remove a section of wall unless they gave him an extremely good reason? It took Lisette all week end to decide to say reluctantly, "All right, Cherry, you may tell him. But make him understand it's *secret.*"

Then Cherry and Lisette had strong misgivings about destroying school property. What right had they to deface Mrs. Harrison's house? None. In fact, the house was also partly the property of the Riverton Bank, which held a mortgage.

"But if we find Pierre's cupboard and the formula," Lisette argued shakily, "maybe we can earn something toward the mortgage installment. Besides, Mrs. Harrison as owner of the chateau has rights in the formula which is hidden in the chateau. You see? So let's go ahead."

Cherry knew she had no right to deface that wall, but she tried to ease her conscience with this thought, "After all, it's just nine unused inches or so inside a closet—our work won't even show."

"So all you have to do," Lisett said finally, "is to persuade Dr. Alan to remove the plaster for us."

"All!" Cherry groaned.

When next she saw Dr. Alan, she put the proposition to him. Or rather, she approached the proposal sideways, holding her breath.

"I was wondering if you'd be willing to do a lady a favor."

"Why, sure," said Alan. "You name it, the Wilcoxes do it."

Cherry did not risk naming the request without cushioning Alan against the shock.

"We—ell. Remember when we had the two injured men to take care of? You offered to lift them or turn them for me. Remember?"

"That's right. I said I'd do the heavy work."

"Yes! Heavy work!"

Alan grinned. "I catch on. What's the heavy work you want me to do?"

Cherry gulped, tried to say "Knock out a wall," and lost her nerve.

"What's the matter? Is it such an awful chore?"

"Yes. It's so awful you'll probably never consent."

"Try me."

"Would you—ah—take a little plastering out of the infirmary closet?"

"How much is *a little* plastering? Did Mrs. Harrison say okay? What's it all about?"

Cherry, of course, gave honest answers.

Alan was dumfounded.

"Well, I'll be darned! And poor Alicia Harrison hasn't any idea that you're planning to tear her house down."

"Oh, not the entire house. But seriously, this perfume thing has real possibilities. Aren't you curious about what we may find after all these years?"

"Yes, I am," Alan said. "Like opening old King Tutankhamen's tomb, hmm? We may find buried scent bottles and the mummified body of old Pierre."

"Don't! That's horrifying!"

"All I'm saying is the Egyptians buried old King Tut in the shadow of the Sphinx with *flacons* of perfume, *perfume,* hear? And when archaeologists dug up the tomb three thousand years later, those *flacons* still gave forth a fragrance. Yes, sir, there's still a chance for old Pierre's sweet-smelling stuff."

"I shouldn't have expected a man to take perfume seriously," Cherry said, half indignant. "But you don't have to laugh at Lisette and me. Perfume is an immense industry—"

"Relax. I know it."

"—and besides, Doctor, scents are added to medicines so they'll smell and taste pleasant enough to swallow."

Alan was able to tell her something more interesting than that. Doctors were originally priests, in ancient times, and they used incense in temples and fragrant healing oils for the sick. In China and India, too, odorous woods and grasses were used and enjoyed. Perfume could be traced back to the very beginning of civilization.

"Besides, just think," Alan said, "of what a lot the Bible says about frankincense and myrrh, and I think aloes. Not to mention honey and fragrant spices like cinnamon."

"And balm of Gilead."

Cherry felt relieved to hear Alan consider seriously the eternal romance of perfume. He could tease all he wanted, but when the question was put, he agreed to do the chore. One thing troubled Dr. Alan—what Mrs. Harrison would say, if she ever found out.

"Looks as if we're going to tear out a piece of a wall on the basis of nothing more than a hollow sound. . . . All right, Cherry, all right! I *said* I'll be there tomorrow night."

Cherry asked him to arrive at five minutes past eight, because beginning at eight o'clock, the school was putting on an amateur theatrical in the gymnasium, which was in a building at a good distance from the chateau. All the students and staff planned to attend, even the telephone calls would be routed over there. The chateau would be deserted, except for the nurse who presumably would be taking care of Lisette's sudden and convenient symptoms.

Alan was as good as his word. He arrived exactly at eight-five, kit in hand and a gleam in his eye. The kit contained less medical tools than (apparently) burglar's tools, or so Lisette remarked as Dr. Alan unpacked a small chisel and saw on Cherry's empty table. Lisette was rather awed at having not only her good friend, Cherry, to help her but also another young grownup.

"You're both very, very kind to do this for me," Lisette said.

"I'm doing it for Cherry," Alan announced. Then he gave Lisette's flying hair a tug. "Glad to help you out, youngster. Just remember who's your friend at court."

"We'd better stop fooling around and get to work!" Cherry warned them. "The coast is clear, but let's not dawdle."

Another reason they had decided on this evening was because Mrs. Harrison was going out to a friend's house for a dinner party. She had left before eight, stately and resplendent in evening attire, and was not expected back before twelve, since the friends lived at some distance.

"I hope she has such a wonderful time that she stays longer," Lisette said. They all rolled up their sleeves and took off their wrist watches. "Now can we start?"

The two girls led Alan to the closet and propped up flashlights to work by. They showed him the section of plaster wall which they wanted him to remove. He gave a low whistle and clapped his forehead.

"It's solid plaster! Do you realize how long it will take?"

"It's now or never," Lisette wailed.

Cherry, huddled in the walk-in closet with the other two, reached out to the supply table for a hammer and chisel. Elbowing her way between Alan and Lisette, she said, "Excuse me," and started chipping away at the offending wall.

"Not that way," Alan said. "Too slow." He showed her how.

"Oh! What are we going to answer," Lisette demanded, "if anyone comes back from the gym and knocks and asks what's the noise and why is the infirmary door locked?"

"As the nurse in charge, I'll go to the door and cope. Somehow."

"Lisette, relax! You have a nurse and a doctor here," said Alan. "Cherry, my beautiful, you're chipping powdered plaster into my hair."

"Sorry. Unavoidable. Ker-choo!"

"That's what you're doing to me, Alan, lower down," Lisette said in a muffled voice.

They worked in a scrambled, hasty fashion, in a cloud of white dust, as fast as six hands would go. From time to time Alan took a sounding to see how they were progressing. In places it was so hard that it took Alan's sharp surgical steel knife to penetrate it and force an opening wedge. Lisette sniffed repeatedly, as if she hoped the cupboard—if it were hidden there—might give off its old perfume. When Cherry's chisel struck wood, the three of them gave a muted cheer. But they cheered too soon. Alan's chisel, up high as he stood on a chair, and Lisette's chisel down low as she knelt, also struck wood, but only here and there.

For a few minutes they were stymied. Surely the wood was not the medicine cabinet itself. It covered too large a space and was not a solid, unbroken area of wood.

Alan said, with his ear against the gap torn out of the plaster, "The sound of it— That doesn't echo the way an outside wall would. Too thin. That's lathing under this plaster!"

They hacked away furiously at the remaining plaster. As they dug deeper, wood lathing became visible in places. Cherry hastily swept up the big chunks of plaster and wiped up some of the powdered plaster. She and Alan and Lisette still had to remove the lathing. The lathing came out awkwardly but without real trouble. Alan trundled pieces of it out of the closet and Cherry trained her flashlight on the newly opened end of the closet. Under the flashlight's beam shone diamond-shaped panes of rose, purple, green, and amber.

"We've found the missing window!"

Alan popped in to see. "Hey, look!" he exclaimed.

"The cupboard!" Lisette jumped up and down in her excitement. "The cupboard—it *is*, isn't it?"

In a sizable wall niche, directly under the diamond-shaped window, was a built-in cupboard with a door. Its top was rounded, and it was made entirely of painted wood. In its door was an old brass keyhole.

"The doll's key!" Lisette sputtered. "The doll's in the same drawer, Cherry, isn't she?"

"Hush! Someone's knocking on the infirmary door!" Cherry exclaimed.

The three of them stood as if frozen. The rapping was light but insistent. Cherry glanced in panic at her watch lying on a shelf—ten o'clock, it read. Maybe a student was knocking. She pushed back her black curls, shakily unlocked the door, and prayed.

If Pierre's ghost had stood there waiting to enter, it would not have given Cherry a nastier turn than the sight of a golden-haired lady in a long sapphire-velvet gown. Mrs. Harrison still wore her long gloves and wrap; she must have just come home—early.

"Why is the infirmary door locked? And what is that odd, dusty smell?"

The headmistress walked in—Cherry had no way of stopping her. At her back was the closet, wide-open and telltale, with the two other conspirators hiding inside it. Cherry endeavored to keep Mrs. Harrison's back toward the closet.

"Won't you sit down? *Here,* Mrs. Harrison?"

"No, thank you. Why, everything seems to be covered with a fine white powder." The headmistress eyed

Cherry's hair. "What *is* going on in here, Cherry?"

Then the headmistress turned around. She saw the mess and destruction, and gave a little shriek. Alan chose this moment to step out of the closet.

"Alan Wilcox! You? Not on a medical call? What are you doing here at such a late hour?" Mrs. Harrison was distressed. "Where is your judgment, Alan? And your manners?"

"I'm sorry, Mrs. Harrison—we can explain—"

Lisette eased herself out of the closet, an elf whose hair and face were covered with chalky blotches. It would have been funny had not Mrs. Harrison been so upset—so very angry.

"Never mind explanations! How can any of you explain destroying a house—a house which doesn't belong to you! Lisette, of all ungrateful children—"

"Please believe me, we're doing it for a good reason—to help you, too—"

Cherry could not think of any reasonable explanation with Mrs. Harrison speaking scornful, stinging words. Her scorn hurt less than her distress; Alicia Harrison actually looked as if she might cry. Cherry suddenly realized the enormity of what she had done.

"Please, please, listen to our reasons," Lisette begged. The girl stepped forward and produced the old journal. "Mrs. Harrison, this is the diary of my great-grandfather, Pierre Gauthier. Would you be kind enough to look at this page? And perhaps this one?"

Mrs. Harrison accepted the journal and read, frowning a little. "The handwriting's difficult— Lisette, please translate these two words."

"A concealed cupboard," Lisette read, while Alan and Cherry looked at each other. "May I tell you the entire story, please, *please?*"

Mrs. Harrison sighed and sat down in a subdued way. Her anger had evaporated. While Lisette recounted the story of the lost perfume, Cherry noticed that the headmistress listened as if deeply moved. Once she broke in to say:

"Yes, yes, I remember how my own grandmother used to bring the fragrance of the garden into our house. Practically every woman knew how to keep herself and her household dainty, with materials from her garden. We all learned how to make sachets for our linen closets and dressers."

Alan and Cherry were glad to see her so interested and sympathetic to the general subject of perfume. Mrs. Harrison smiled reminiscently and promised to show Lisette and Cherry how to mix dried rose petals with sugar and spices to make a lasting potpourri. Lisette tactfully drew the headmistress's attention back to the great-grandfather's lasting scent, and in particular to his formula.

"What about his formula? Was it for a poor old man's hobby that you three young idiots tore out a wall?"

"But the formula is so much more than an old man's hobby," Lisette insisted. "Mrs. Harrison, we can't stop now! I don't know just how to say it, to make you see—"

"You mean, I suppose, that you are so deeply involved you must finish what you've started? Ordinarily I would say that's a good, conscientious attitude. But, Lisette, what makes you think Pierre Gauthier's perfume formula is any good?"

"No one ever believed in Great-grandfather's formula, but I do!"

"How do you *know*—not merely believe sentimentally and blindly, but *know*—that the formula actually creates a fine perfume?"

Lisette looked stricken. Cherry tried to come to her rescue.

"Pierre Gauthier's garden flowers are wonderfully fragrant, Mrs. Harrison. The special roses and the silver lace—"

"The perfume may not resemble the flowers at all," Mrs. Harrison pointed out. "Even if your great-grandfather Pierre used those flowers in making his perfume, a chemical change during the process could alter the flowers' fragrance entirely. Isn't that correct, Dr. Alan?"

"Yes, that's right, Mrs. Harrison. Odor depends on invisible molecules and their organic structure. If you crush a rose petal, you change the structure and possibly the fragrance."

"There, you see! Lisette, you are dreaming."

Alan cleared his throat. "Well, it's a funny thing about odors, Mrs. Harrison. Odor," he said, "defies chemical explanation. Chemistry *plus something unknown* make a scent what it is. Chemistry and mathematics together cannot analyze, for instance, a violet. So you see, Mrs. Harrison, there's a fifty-fifty chance for any reasonably skilled perfume formula."

Lisette looked as if she could hug him. Cherry beamed at him. Mrs. Harrison leaned back in her chair, saying she was open to reason.

"Just give me a chance to prove it *is* a lovely scent," Lisette cried.

"Since you have gone this far in the search, I will not stop you now. I myself would be very happy if the formula could be found and if it worked out well."

Still, she was dubious. She looked so worried, so tired in her splendid dress, that Cherry realized what a burden they were putting on her, had been putting on her, all along.

"Mrs. Harrison?" Cherry ventured. "We—we thought you knew or guessed what we were up to."

The lady smiled. "I knew Lisette was prowling, and I thought you were, too, Cherry, but I trusted you." They felt immensely grateful to her for that. "So I didn't pay much attention. I've had school finances so much on my mind, as you know—"

Lisette boldly said, "The perfume formula might earn something for the school. If we find it." Her glance strayed to the open closet.

"My dear Lisette, I hope your dream comes true, and you are sweet to think of the school. We would have to discuss anything of that sort. But there is a time limit on your dream. Yes, go ahead with whatever you have found. I'm interested, in spite of my better judgment."

"It's Pierre Gauthier's cupboard in there!" Lisette told her.

Mrs. Harrison nodded and it struck Cherry that the headmistress accepted all these extraordinary facts without much explanation.

In order to open the cupboard, Lisette went to the bureau drawer and took out the doll. She was busy extracting the key from the doll's little handbag when Mrs. Harrison noticed and exclaimed:

"Where did you find that doll? I haven't seen a doll like that one in years!"

Lisette handed her the little wooden manikin, explaining that it had resided behind the stuck drawer. Then she presented the doll's key to Alan. They all crowded behind the young man, focusing their flashlights, while he tried the key in the cupboard's keyhole.

It fit! Alan turned the key, and with a creak the cupboard door swung open. A strong odor of decaying, cloyingly sweet chemicals floated out to them.

On the cupboard's shelves stood the remains of Pierre's miniature laboratory. Cherry could identify old-fashioned scales and measuring spoons and stirring rods. More important, she saw old, empty bottles and jars whose labels of perfume ingredients were still dimly legible. Finding those labels provided them with valuable information.

"Where is the formula?" Lisette mumbled in her ear.

"I thought you already had the formula," Mrs. Harrison said in some exasperation.

"Part of it is in the journal," Lisette said lamely. "I thought—from one passage in the journal—that Great-grandfather might have left the complete formula here in the cupboard somewhere."

This was a serious lack. Cherry had seen the fragment of the formula in the journal and understood it to a degree with the aid of Lisette's perfume textbook from the library. Though the journal mentioned the Provence, China, and fawn roses and the silver spray, it gave no clue to the all-important thing—which flower was the *key* to the perfume.

Cherry hastily figured. First, the journal hinted strongly at the existence of further notes. A second thing: from her own nursing training, Cherry knew that any scientist experimenting in a laboratory records his findings in a laboratory book of some sort. Such a record book naturally belongs with the lab equipment; it was not likely that Pierre carried his working notes around in his pocket.

These two facts made Cherry suspect that further notes must have existed, and might still exist. If they were not actually *in* the cupboard, might they not be near it? Would these notes be written on scraps of paper, or would they be written as systematically as the diary? In fact, Cherry wondered, mightn't the notes be written in a largish, leather-bound notebook similar to the personal journal?

"Hmm! But that's too big to fit into the cupboard! In that case—"

"What's too big, Cherry?"

She was too busy to answer them. Cherry ran her hand along the newly revealed wall. She was probing for a hidden drawer or ledge or even a wall safe which might hold a second journal. But she found nothing. She walked slowly through the long, narrow supply closet with its shallow shelves of linens and nursing equipment, and trained her flashlight's beam up, down, and around. On the closet ceiling the square outline of a trap door caught her attention.

"Alan! Would you bring a chair, please? Let's try that trap door." She held the light steady so the others could see.

"There's nothing up there, Cherry," said Mrs. Harrison. She explained that in these flat-roofed Victorian houses there were no attics, only a few feet of air space or at most a very low, unfinished garret in which a person could only crouch. These few feet served only for ventilation and insulation.

Cherry said politely, "If you don't object, it might not hurt to have a look, anyhow."

For there was a chance that old Pierre, jealous of his perfume secrets, feeling alone in a not-too-understanding household, might have kept his formula notes in a safe hiding place. A bureau drawer or a wall cupboard could be invaded, but an inconspicuous ceiling trap door was fairly safe.

Alan brought the chair and, as he was the tallest, climbed up and pushed until the trap door moved. Lisette handed him a wooden ruler with which to prop the trap door open. Alan reached up and felt around with both hands.

"Nothing up here but cobwebs and dust—can't see a thing. Wait, I think I touched something."

"Want a flashlight?" Cherry asked.

"Never mind, I have it, whatever it is."

Covered with dust, hardly recognizable, it was a crumbling, largish, flat, leather-bound notebook which Alan handed down. Cherry and Lisette wiped it off with dampened paper towels. Mrs. Harrison murmured that she was glad Pierre Gauthier had not relegated the charming little doll to the ceiling trap door and all that dust, but Cherry scarcely heard. She and Lisette could hardly believe their luck and relief at finding a second notebook. Its pages bore Pierre's spidery, Spencerian handwriting, as did his personal journal, but these pages were filled with formulas and directions.

"In French," Alan remarked, reading over their shoulders. He had washed, and was drying, his hands. "Will you look at that! *Grammes, litres,* and what's this mean? *Ajouter ensuite 500 centimétres cubes d'eau*—"

"I can interpret it," Lisette insisted. "After all, when I found Pierre's personal journal in Papa's old trunk, I figured it out with the French dictionary. I'll figure out this second journal with the perfume textbook."

Curiously enough, Mrs. Harrison was not paying any attention to their discovery. She was holding and touching the doll. She did not look up even when Lisette, excitedly leafing through the pages of the formulary, exclaimed:

"I think this is it! I *think* this is the key information!" She translated haltingly, " 'The base is silver lace, yet my creation is a rosy odor, for which I depend chiefly on my Provence rose!' "

Mrs. Harrison walked to the doorway and paused, still holding the old doll. "I think, for reasons of my own, I shall keep this little creature," she said.

Tears stood in her eyes, Cherry saw, just before Mrs. Harrison turned away and left. She thought she saw tears in Lisette's young eyes as well.

CHAPTER XI

# *Experiment*

A BURST OF LAUGHTER SOUNDED OUTSIDE THE INfirmary door. It sounded to Cherry as if the entire student body of the Jamestown School were scrambling and chattering from open doors all down the hall. Friday afternoons were always a bedlam. Over three portable phonographs playing like mad, Sibyl shouted:

"None of you care about me the tiniest little bit! Won't somebody run down and mail this note for me?"

"Oh, Sib, we're busy! What did Mrs. Harrison say we're supposed to put in next?" That was Francie, one of Sibyl's loyal clique—actually evading the duchess's order.

"Who's using all the ribbon?" That squeal sounded like Jannie, with her mouth full of candy. "Honestly! Give me some more of the pink and rose."

"Gee, these are going to look darling."

From down the hall Nancy called, "Who wants to cram with me for the monthly torture quizzes?"

Somebody called back, "Later, Nan—this sachet deal is getting glamorous."

Cherry smiled as she worked in the infirmary and reflected that she wouldn't mind making a sachet herself. Mrs. Harrison had described how to do it the other evening, in the sitting room, instead of reading poetry for them as she often did. The process was simple but made a most attractive gift:

Choose a chiffon handkerchief in a pastel color and in its center place a mixture of dried lavender flowers, rose-geranium leaves, rose petals, and a few crushed leaves of lemon verbena. Then tie up the handkerchief with ribbons in colors representing the contents. These sachets were to be placed in with one's garments and writing paper, and lent a dainty fragrance.

Cherry had thought Lisette would be encouraged at this proof of the headmistress's interest in the subject of scents. But Lisette was annoyed because many of the girls begged roses and leaves from the conservatory just when every blossom might be needed to compound Pierre's perfume.

"Besides," Lisette had protested to Cherry, "we don't want the whole school to get so interested in perfumes —or they'll guess what we're up to in the infirmary."

Cherry and Lisette were doing their best to keep the experiment a secret, chiefly because they wanted to avoid time-consuming interruptions. So far this week the two girls had accomplished a good deal. They had set up an improvised chemistry laboratory on a spare enamel-topped table, using the infirmary's electric stove, rubber tubing, saucepans, kettles, and glass jars and bottles. Both girls were studying the perfume textbook intensively. ("The library fine on this book will be a ransom, even if I did take it for two months," Lisette said. But Alan promised to try to renew the book's time limit for her when next he went to Riverton.) Alan had ordered for them, through his physician's contacts with chemical supply houses, certain of the perfume ingredients such as ninety per cent alcohol. Cherry had ordered from a perfumery supply house, by mail, one very expensive ounce of extract of ilang-ilang, which means "flower of flowers," a yellowish-green flower grown in Burma, and which Pierre's formula required. In addition, Cherry and Lisette had pieced together Pierre's formula, until it seemed to them and to Alan to appear complete and reasonable. Of course, no one ever knew about anything as volatile and unpredictable as perfume. By the end of the week all of their ingredients, equipment, and notes were assembled. Now Cherry and Lisette were ready actually to try out the precious, questionable formula.

Saturday was their great chance. The chateau was quiet and nearly deserted this sunny morning. Virtually the entire school had gone off on their horses for an overnight trip to River's End and the lodge. Lisette, who was a good horsewoman, would not have missed this trip for anything, excepting this was the perfect chance to experiment. Cherry had been invited, too, but chose loyally to remain with Lisette. Also, she was bursting with curiosity to find out how Pierre's formula would work.

"Or whether we can *make* it work," Cherry said under her breath. She rigged up the apparatus and plugged in the small electric stove.

Lisette came in with her garden basket filled with silver lace and the three types of roses she had just picked. The girl's hands shook as she stripped off the petals.

"Do you think we can really distill out the flowers' essential oils, Cherry?"

"Certainly. There's no special trick to that part. It would go faster if we had a hospital sterilizer."

The girls worked quickly, knowing that the odor changes as the flowers die. Lisette weighed the petals on the borrowed kitchen scale, translating from Pierre's *grammes* into ounces, and using the proportions noted in Pierre's formula. As she finished weighing each batch, Cherry put the petals into a wire basket or strainer, and placed this in a kettle, adding half as much water as petals. She fit a cork over the spout of the kettle; this cork had a hole cut in it. Into the cork Cherry inserted tubing, about four feet long, while Lisette spread putty around the kettle's spout and lid to make it airtight.

"Now!" said Cherry. "Here we go."

She placed the kettle full of petals and water in a large saucepan of boiling water on the stove. Lisette took the free end of the tubing and placed it in a small open jar which was set away from the stove, and lower than the stove. Cherry brought a pan of cold water and coiled the tubing in it, where the tubing ran between kettle and jar.

"I can smell it already," Lisette said hopefully.

A delicious fragrance of blended flowers began to fill the infirmary, as the water in the kettle heated and vaporized into steam. What happened was this: the vapor passed through the mass of petals, became chilled as it passed through the cold tubing, and condensed into small drops that fell into the open jar. These drops were the essential natural oils which gave the flowers their fragrance. It took two hours to complete the distillation, and it took patience.

"Did you notice," Lisette asked Cherry, "that the air in here, while it smells nice, doesn't smell exactly like the fresh flowers did? Roses can be distilled but maybe silver lace can't. The textbook doesn't mention silver lace—"

"Now don't start worrying. We have to allow for changes due to the distillation, and correct it later with chemicals."

Following the instructions of the perfume text, the girls removed the glass jar with its distillate—the precious key to Pierre's perfume—covered it, and set it aside. In three or four hours the essential oils would rise and float on the surface of the water in the jar. The girls cleaned and put away this part of their equipment and went downstairs for lunch. They could hardly tell what they were eating; everything tasted of roses. Apparently some of the natural flower oils had clung to their hands.

That afternoon Cherry and Lisette carefully skimmed off the oil in the jar, using a spoon at first until Cherry had the bright idea of using an eye dropper. They transferred the oil to a small, clean amber bottle, filled it to the top with flower oil, and sealed the bottle with hot paraffin.

"The book says, 'Store in a cool, dark place,' " Lisette read.

"Well, what about the infirmary's little refrigerator?"

"Then all the medicines will taste of flowers," Lisette giggled.

"Oops! Don't throw away that water that's left in the jar."

Lisette sniffed it. "But of course. It's rose water. We have a perfectly nice cologne here. If we add a little pink or lavender coloring, it would *seem* more fragrant—"

"We can't stop now to tint toilet water, Lisette. We're racing against perishable flower oils."

Now all the thinking and studying and pondering of Pierre's formula, which they had done during these past days, helped them to act with dispatch. Luckily for them, the old formula called for chemicals and perfumers' synthetics which were still in use and which, like the alcohol base, Alan had obtained for them. This was necessary because several other ingredients beside the essential flower oils were needed to create a finished perfume. Lisette read aloud, translating Pierre's old formula as they had pieced it together from the two journals:

"Over a period of a week, preferably, infuse 7 litres of 90 per cent alcohol with:

| | | |
|---|---|---|
| Distilled rose water .................. | 5 | *litres* |
| Extract of commercial orange flower water ............................ | 3 | " |
| Essence (in equal parts) of fawn, China and Provence roses ................. | 200 | *grammes* |
| Essence of silver lace ................. | 110 | " |
| Essence of bitter almonds ............. | 20 | " |
| Essence of bergamot .................. | 25 | " |
| Vanillin ............................ | 15 | " |

Fixative? Musk? Balsam?
Add 500 centimetres of water, set aside, filter.

Lisette had already arranged for their doing the job more swiftly than in seven days. She allowed for differences between commercial ingredients of her great-grandfather's time and of her own (such as the synthetic artificial essences of bitter almond and bergamot). Houbigant, who had made perfumed gloves for Napoleon Bonaparte, had adapted ancient recipes with modern chemicals, so Lisette and Cherry, given this great precedent, dared to be hopeful.

The two girls did some extremely exact measuring, considering that an ounce equals 28.35 *grammes,* and a *litre* equals 1.76 pint. They scaled down Pierre's formula to the tiny amount of perfume they were making, for they had only one small bottle of the natural flower oil with which to experiment. They took the flower oil out of the refrigerator. To this flower oil they added, carefully, the other ingredients of the formula, exactly as the textbook directed. Such concentration was tiring. As they worked and the afternoon lengthened, Cherry wished Dr. Alan would look in. He had promised to try to do so. They could use a third pair of hands and some encouragement. Finally Cherry and Lisette added a little fixative which, of a retiring odor itself, would make the perfume lasting.

"I'm almost afraid to sniff what we've made," Lisette admitted. She looked tired.

"We have to remember that a perfume needs a chance to ripen. Anyway, we've been smelling so many scents all day long," Cherry said, "I suspect we have 'odor fatigue.' We can't judge this new perfume now."

"I can't wait!"

"We ought to wait a week. Poor Lisette. Let's wait three days, at least."

Cherry put away the bottle of finished perfume, tightly stoppered, on a high shelf to ripen.

The following three days were the hardest Cherry could remember. Somehow, word leaked out among the girls that she and Lisette were trying to make a new perfume, and the teasing added to their unease. Sibyl said scornfully, "Why should amateurs bother, when you can go out and buy the most magnificent perfumes?" All Lisette could reply was, "Why bother ever to do anything new and original?" She tried to explain to Sibyl that there was no *one* true odor of rose and no perfume at all of the rare silver lace, but Sibyl flounced off without listening.

"It's enough to make one cry," Lisette complained to Cherry. "I wonder what Mrs. Harrison is thinking?"

Tuesday finally arrived. The three days were up. The two girls asked Dr. Alan to come over, but Lisette lacked the courage to invite Mrs. Harrison.

Late Tuesday afternoon Cherry, Alan, and Lisette closed the infirmary door and took the bottle of Pierre's perfume down from the shelf. Cherry sniffed first and could not trust her own senses. She tried to keep her face expressionless for Lisette's sake. Then Lisette sniffed the bottle; then she applied a little of the perfume to her wrist and to a clean blotter, and sniffed again.

"For gosh sake!" Alan blurted out. "It's nothing in particular—I can smell that much even at a distance."

Lisette sank into a chair and tears ran down her face. Alan patted her shoulder. Cherry wanted to console her, but what could she say? The perfume's ingredients just did not blend. Discounting the rawness of the chemicals, which time would improve, all they had here was a mixture of awfully sweet odors. These did not harmonize into a perfume at all.

"I don't believe it!" Lisette stormed. "I don't believe Pierre's perfume was as hopeless as this! It's *our* fault, not his. We did something wrong!"

"Let's analyze your possible errors step by step," Alan said calmly. Cherry, because of her training in the sciences, led off. Could they have pieced the formula together incorrectly? On checking back, they did not think so. Had they used a fixative which drowned out the flower odors? No, they could discern each separate flower scent. Had distillation ruined the essential oil of the silver lace? Should they have used a more delicate method? No, they could discern a scent resembling silver lace even in the ruined perfume.

"Maybe we were *too* exact," Lisette muttered, "and too scientific. After all, perfume making is an art as well as a science. If we try again, we'll depend on our noses as well as the formula."

"You'll try again," Alan encouraged her. He looked uncertain, but soothed her, saying they would surely think of some solution. It was only kindness on his part, for when he said good-by to Cherry in the hall, he admitted:

"I have no idea what to do next. Have you?"

"No. I mean, not yet." Cherry jammed her hands in her uniform pockets. "I'll think of something, though."

"I'll bet you will. If I can help, let me know."

As if this disappointment were not enough, Lisette was in a bad state of mind about what Mrs. Harrison would say.

"I can't bear to tell her that we've failed. Here we've torn a gaping hole in the closet, and stripped the conservatory bare—and we've failed!"

"We won't give up too soon," Cherry said grimly. "We're beaten this time, but there's always a next time. Give me a day or two to think."

"Mrs. Harrison will lose all respect for me. I tell you, Cherry, I wouldn't be surprised if she canceled my scholarship and sent me home!"

"Now, Lisette, stop talking nonsense."

Lisette started to cry so helplessly that Cherry heard only snatches of seemingly unreasonable things. "My own mother doesn't believe in Pierre's formula, so why should Mrs. Harrison? Oh, I can't bear it!"

The next day a rumor started among the girls that Lisette was Mrs. Harrison's niece.

Cherry heard the rumor and did not like its unpleasant undertone. The gossip hinted that as the headmistress's niece, Lisette enjoyed special privileges. Cherry knew this was not true. If anything, Mrs. Harrison was rather stricter and more impersonal with Lisette than with the other girls, probably in an effort *not* to favor her.

The way the rumor took hold was appalling. Sibyl's older clique, Cora, Francie, and Susan, addressed Lisette in dripping tones as "pet." Someone stuck a sign on the stripped conservatory: *Private.* Even good-natured Nancy, when she and little Mary gave a hot-chocolate party in their room, left Lisette out, conspicuously.

If the headmistress was aware of the gossip, she gave no indication of it. Lisette maintained her dignity in the dining room, but Mademoiselle and Mr. North reported in the faculty room that the girl seemed nervous in class. "When *ma petite* Lisette stumbles in her French lesson," declared Mlle. Gabriel, "maybe she should consult the nurse."

Lisette stood the embarrassment for most of the week, then burst into the infirmary at lunch hour on Friday.

"Cherry, do I have to face those cats again? I'd rather go hungry. Let me stay here with you."

Cherry was lunching upstairs in order to keep an eye on Jannie, who was trying to ward off laryngitis. She had given Jannie prescribed medication and a lunch of hot liquids, and now had made her comfortable for an afternoon nap. This done, Cherry took Lisette into her own adjoining room, leaving the door open in case her patient needed her.

Lisette talked in whispers. Cherry recalled the incident in the infirmary when she had sensed "that something complex existed here." The whole story spilled out.

It was true that Lisette was Alicia Harrison's niece. They had kept this fact in the background in order to save embarrassment. And now poor Mrs. Harrison had to endure all these unkind thoughts and remarks! Lisette was a great deal more distressed for her aunt than for herself. Cherry tried to listen with a double awareness for what connection all of this might have with the perfume project.

Alicia Harrison was the granddaughter of Pierre Gauthier, and the daughter of Pierre's only child, Louis. Louis had also had a son, Gilbert, who was Lisette's late father. Alicia had grown up here in the Chateau Larose. She had married a Richard Harrison and resided with him in New York until his death left her a widow. In the meantime, Gilbert married Lisette's mother and they, too, lived for some years in New York. After Lisette's grandfather and grandmother died, the Chateau Larose was untenanted by any members of the family, until her aunt took over the Jamestown School.

"Aunt Alicia has never had any idea why I wanted so badly to come here. She awarded me the scholarship out of the goodness of her heart. Oh, yes, certainly, she knew about Pierre's dabbling in perfumes. But like the rest of the family, she didn't take it too seriously."

"Did she know about Pierre's diary?" Cherry asked.

"I'm not sure, but I don't think so. Papa had taken it years ago as a kind of curiosity and buried it in a trunk. But I'm sure of this much. Aunt Alicia never guessed her own school building held a secret."

Now that Mrs. Harrison did finally know about Pierre's perfume, Lisette said in despair, they had failed.

"My own mother laughs—and now I suppose Aunt Alicia will too, at my childhood dream. Mother's always said, 'Lisette, your imagination is running away with you.' " She sighed. "Cherry, do you know what I dread most, right now? More gossip! If the girls unearth the fact that we've failed—"

"You feel that would embarrass Mrs. Harrison still more?"

There were many more puzzling facets of the story—so many questions on the tip of Cherry's tongue—but the warning bell rang for the first afternoon class. Lisette had to run. She hesitated in the hall doorway.

"Did you see, Cherry, how even the old doll with its memories affected Aunt Alicia? Now all this horrid meddling talk. Of all darling people to be gossiped about!"

The girl fled. She left Cherry feeling very much troubled. Mrs. Harrison needed help and could not herself, without loss of dignity, track down whoever had started the talk. But Cherry had a good idea who had done it.

One girl in particular held a grudge against Mrs. Harrison. That girl, only a few days ago, again had been called into the headmistress's office for a disciplinary talk, for one of her repeated infractions of school rules. That girl was Sibyl. Cherry knew Sibyl held a grudge against her, too, suspecting Cherry had scared away her precious Freddie.

"Well," Cherry decided, "sooner or later this situation with Miss Troublemaker has to come to a head."

She went downstairs to look for Sibyl among the girls who were leaving the dining room. Sibyl was nowhere to be seen. The open door of Mrs. Harrison's office gave Cherry a better idea.

The headmistress was not in her pleasant office-study,

but Cherry found Mrs. Curtis there. In addition to her teaching duties, she assisted Mrs. Harrison with the administrative work. She looked up coolly as the young nurse came in.

Cherry explained what she wanted to know.

"That is a shrewd guess, Miss Ames," said Mrs. Curtis. "Ordinarily neither Mrs. Harrison nor I give out such information. Can you tell me why you need to know?"

Cherry explained this, too. She was so determined that her crisp white nurse's cap trembled atop her black curls.

"Very well, Miss Ames. As you are aware, Sibyl was called into this office the other evening. She had left library books lying on the porch in the rain—but that is not the point. While Sibyl was in here, both Mrs. Harrison and I were called into the library for a few minutes. Sibyl was left alone in this office. I distinctly recall that a letter from Lisette's mother was lying open on Mrs. Harrison's desk, and I am very much afraid that Sibyl read it."

"I suppose she was attracted by the name Gauthier on the envelope or letterhead," Cherry said. And Sibyl had disliked Lisette ever since the fiasco of her "stolen" lapis lazuli bracelet.

"The letter which Sibyl read, without any right to do so," Mrs. Curtis said, "did reveal that Lisette is Alicia Harrison's niece. A few of us instructors knew that, but we felt it was a private matter, and no need for the students to know of the relationship. Sibyl certainly is making capital of it!"

Cherry thanked Mrs. Curtis and wrote a note to Sibyl asking her to stop by the infirmary and slipped it under the door. Then she went back to her work. When Sibyl did not put in an appearance by late afternoon, Cherry decided to seek her out. She met her in the upstairs corridor.

"Didn't you find my note that I want to see you?"

Sibyl shrugged. She had ignored the note.

"Sibyl, was it you who spread this talk about Lisette being the headmistress's niece?"

"It's true. What if I did spill the beans?"

"You're a born mischief-maker. Aren't you ashamed of what you've stirred up?"

"Why should I be? I'm bored to death seeing that privileged character hang around the infirmary at all hours, doing heaven knows what! A lot of the other girls resent it, too."

"Yes, because you've deliberately created resentment and ill feeling." Cherry's eyes snapped. "You saw your chance to hurt Mrs. Harrison and you took it, didn't you?"

"Do some people bore you, Miss Ames?" Sibyl said insolently, and strolled away.

Mrs. Harrison must have learned that Cherry had unmasked Sibyl as the gossipmonger; probably Sibyl, who enjoyed attention of any sort, publicized it herself. For the next evening during dinner, Mrs. Harrison asked for silence, saying she had something to tell the assembled girls.

All around the candlelit tables, and at the headmistress's long table, students and faculty members stopped talking. All faces turned toward the beautiful woman. Cherry noticed that Lisette, seated with the younger girls, looked pale but confident.

"There is something I would like all of you to know," Mrs. Harrison said pleasantly. "Word has been circulating that Lisette Gauthier is my niece, and of course that is quite true. Lisette is my late brother's daughter. I cannot imagine why any of you should really care whether we are aunt and niece or not. If it is a matter of Lisette's scholarship, you might like to know that two other girls—who are not related to me—have scholarships, too. My entire effort has been not to favor any girl, nor"—the headmistress glanced at Sibyl—"to show disfavor to any girl even when there is the provocation. It was this desire to be fair and impartial to *all* you girls, you see, which was the reason for my not announcing that Lisette is my niece. I've tried very hard, and I think you can see for yourselves that I haven't favored Lisette or anyone else."

A murmur went around the dining room. It was sympathetic. Sibyl's face had turned nearly as red as her hair, but she sat staring boldly at the headmistress.

"The interesting part of the story," Mrs. Harrison continued serenely, "has to do with this house, which as you know is the Chateau Larose."

Across the room Cherry and Lisette exchanged startled glances. Was Mrs. Harrison going to give away their secret? The perfume experiment still was unfinished—

"My grandfather built this house after a French design of his era and planted the garden with rare seeds from France. He built it for his wife, although she did not live many years after their son, Louis, my father, was born. The Chateau Larose was occupied by our family until several years ago, when my parents—Lisette's grandparents—died. The chateau was left to me, as the elder child. I leased it, with all its original furniture, to some people who founded the Jamestown School here. That is why, incidentally, Lisette never saw the chateau until she came to the school this fall. Then, five years ago, I decided to take over the school. I thought you girls would like to know that the house has a long and romantic history."

She turned aside and asked the waitress for more coffee. Her announcement was over.

She had not said a word about the chateau's secret! Cherry and Lisette smiled at each other in relief. Nor had Mrs. Harrison spoken out against the girl who had manufactured the trouble.

In the sitting room after dinner, the other girls drifted away from Sibyl, even Francie, Cora, and Susan, but she aggressively strolled after them.

"Why, chicks, you were the first to listen when I told you the tidbit," Sibyl wheedled.

"You made us listen but we didn't enjoy it," Francie retorted. The other two members of her one-time clique looked at Sibyl with dwindling respect. She floundered.

"Ho-hum. Stuffy, aren't you? Oh, I forgot to tell you I expect to hear from my darling Freddie any moment now." This remark was met with tight-lipped disbelief.

"I saw Freddie in the village with that local Blair girl," Cora said very clearly.

"Oh, all right!" Sibyl burst out. "You know, anyway, that Freddie hasn't called me for weeks and weeks. As if I cared! As if I cared either, about this tiresome old school!"

She banged out of the room, making a loud if not very grand exit.

A few days later it became generally known that Sibyl had prevailed upon her parents to send her to another school. The reason was obvious: the girls at the Jamestown School no longer took her seriously, and some of them were snubbing her. Mrs. Harrison handled the unfortunate situation tactfully. She remarked to several groups of girls:

"Sibyl's parents and I have talked the matter over, and we agree that a change of school is in order."

That was all the headmistress said, but Sibyl's defeat was complete, and no one was too sorry that she was leaving.

On the day she left she came into the infirmary looking for Lisette and Cherry. In her hand she carried, gingerly, the lapis lazuli bracelet.

"Miss Ames, I—I just want to say I hope you haven't any hard feelings toward me."

"Of course not, Sibyl. I hope you'll be happy at the new school and make lots of friends there."

"Oh, I'm sure I will. Lisette? Would you—ah—like to have this bracelet?" It was the closest Sibyl could come to offering an apology. She held out the trinket.

Lisette accepted it without much enthusiasm, but with good grace. Smiling, she said, "It's very nice of you, Sibyl. I shall enjoy wearing it."

Five minutes later Sibyl was driving away in the station wagon. The school would go on without her.

CHAPTER XII

# What Molly Recalled

THE PERFUME EXPERIMENT WAS AT A STANDSTILL UNtil Cherry had an idea. She thought of it as she woke up one morning, and hastened to tell Lisette about it at breakfast time.

"I have a notion of where our experiment went wrong! Aren't those garden flowers we distilled pretty old, neglected plants? Pierre's garden hasn't had any adequate care for years and years. Well, then, maybe the flowers we used have lost their vitality and lost most of their true scent."

Lisette's eyes glinted with new hope. "You mean Great-grandfather worked with healthier, more fragrant flowers than we did? That just might be it!"

Cherry also had another idea, a fairly obvious one. She thought her and Lisette's knowledge of chemistry was not too expert and affected their experiment.

"This time," said Lisette, agreeing, "let's try to have lots more help from Alan. He likes you so much, Cherry, he'd do it for you."

"He'd do it out of interest in the perfume," Cherry countered.

"He *does* like you, Cherry. Haven't you noticed?"

Cherry flushed. She had noticed. As for her own feelings, the longer she knew Alan Wilcox, the better she liked him.

"We were discussing the perfume," Cherry said firmly. "Yes, I will ask Dr. Alan to give us more help, especially with the chemistry part. But it's your perfume formula, Lisette. It's up to you to decide what's the next step."

"Well, the conclusion you just came to sounds to me like the—like the—"

"The McCoy, to coin a phrase. You mean Pierre's neglected flowers have lost most of their vitality and true scent?"

The two girls thought it over all day, and that evening they decided that this was the cause of their failure in re-creating his formula. Possibly there were other factors, too, but worn-out plants were the chief shortcoming. Then the problem became: where to find silver lace and Provence, fawn, and China roses which were as healthy and vividly fragrant as Pierre's originally had been.

"The minister raises a few of those flowers in his garden," Lisette remembered. "Even if we had the courage to ask him, there's nothing growing in his garden in November."

"Has he a conservatory?"

"No. I inquired. He hasn't, and neither have other people around here. Only summer gardens."

"There must be somebody around who has a conservatory or hothouse," Cherry mused. "Of course we might send away to a commercial florist or seed house, but that's not exactly on the right track, is it?"

"I'm afraid not. Great-grandfather's flowers were started from seeds from France, and what he grew was grown *locally*. No, we'll find his flowers right around here or not at all."

"Wait! I think I have it!" Cherry's whole face began to sparkle. "Remember when you and I were stalled in the taxi—that first, hot day we met? Remember the farm woman who came by with a horse and a wagon full of flowers? She had a nursery."

"You're right. Molly Something. Molly Miller. We bought a bouquet from her. It had some silver lace in it, only we didn't know what it was at the time."

Cherry said excitedly, "Remember she invited us to come and see her flowers. Remember? We're going! I don't remember where she lives, but Alan will tell us."

Alan did more than that. He drove Cherry over to Rivers' Crossing. Lisette was unable to go along because of classes. Cherry's duties were waived for her for a few hours through the kindness of Mrs. Harrison.

It was one of those crystal-clear days with a sky so

bright that the bare, blowing branches seemed to be etched against it. Alan had a call to make along the route. That made Cherry feel better about their driving so deep into the country. Today was their first chance in some time to visit together.

"I hope you don't mind Lena being present even though three's a crowd," said Alan. His car was a perfectly real personality to him, though Cherry suspected he did not admit it to very many people.

"I'm almost as fond of Leaping Lena as you are," Cherry said. "I'd recognize her coughs and grunts even if she waked me out of a sound sleep."

"Lena and Cherry, my two favorite girls," Alan joked. "That's no mean compliment. Dad's car is a dowager, elderly, but he gets where he's going. Speaking of going places, Cherry—"

She thought Alan was about to tease her again about those dates they rarely could manage, but the serious side of him came out. It never failed to impress Cherry.

"I undertook an errand on your and Lisette's behalf the other day, on my own hook. Hope I didn't do anything I shouldn't have. When I was in St. Louis it occurred to me to look in the classified telephone directory and see whether there wasn't a perfume manufacturer or wholesaler or distributor or something in St. Louis. Well, I located a perfume manufacturer, a Mr. Clary, and I went to see him."

"Why, Alan! How very kind of you! Clary. Is that a French name?"

"Right. He's of French descent. An awfully nice man. And you know what? I talked to him about old Pierre's formula and he's interested. He wants us to bring him a sample of it, when we're satisfied with how it turns out."

"Alan! You're as good as Santa Claus. I could kiss you!"

"Any time." He turned to grin at her. "Darn it, we're already at Molly Miller's. You owe me a kiss."

"On account of Mr. Clary."

"On account of me!" Alan retorted, as he swung the car off the road and into a dirt driveway.

They parked beside a farmhouse surrounded by immense oaks. A friendly old dog came to meet them, but no one else was in sight.

"Mrs. Miller and her kids must be working in the hothouses. Come around here, Cherry."

Alan led her around the side of the house. From here she could see glistening rows of long, low, glass roofs. When she had met Molly Miller in her wagon that day, Cherry had not realized the woman owned an extensive nursery. To reach the first hothouse, she and Alan walked through a half acre of what must be flower beds in summer. Alan remarked that he had known Molly Miller all his life, like everyone for miles around, although he had not been down to Rivers' Crossing in a very long time.

Molly Miller heard them coming. She hopped out of a low doorway to wave a trowel at them.

"Alan Wilcox! I declare, how you've grown! How's the doctor?"

"My father's fine, thanks. I'm a physician these days, too. How are you?"

"Never better. How these young ones do grow up! Now I swan, I know this young lady from some place. Couldn't very well forget her rosy cheeks." When Cherry reminded her, Molly Miller seized her hand and shook it heartily.

"I'm always pleased to show folks my place. Step right in."

They stooped and went through the low door into the warm, moist air of the first hothouse. Flowers bloomed here in orderly profusion. Some young people working at the other end looked up and waved. Mrs. Miller showed them rows of chrysanthemums and gerardia, and described her methods. Cherry was only mildly interested. She did glimpse roses in the next hothouse, but they did not seem to be the species which she and Lisette needed.

"Mrs. Miller, we're here today on a special errand. Maybe I'm asking for the impossible, but—"

"Nothing's impossible to an experienced gardener, Miss Cherry. You name it and I'll bet we grow it."

"Well, these particular flowers date back a long time."

"So do I." Molly Miller laughed.

"These are really special local flowers, Mrs. Miller. Do you happen to have any fawn or China or Provence roses?" The farm woman stared at her. "Then there's one other flower I want, which you had in a bouquet you sold us. It's a whitish-silver spray—the only name I know for it is silver lace, but that may not be right."

"Silver lace! I haven't heard that name in years! Where on earth did you hear it? And who told you about such a variety as fawn roses?"

Molly Miller was so surprised that she sat down, stood up, and sat down on a box again. Alan grinned, but he was as impressed as Cherry was.

"Upon my soul, young lady, the last person who *honestly* knew about silver lace and your special roses was old Pierre Gauthier, who started the original plants."

"You knew him!" Cherry exclaimed.

"Yes, I met the old gentleman a few times, but mostly I knew *of* him. Ah, me! You're almost making me see ghosts."

"Care to tell us a ghost story?" Alan asked her. "Seriously, I think Cherry would appreciate hearing about him and his flowers."

"Sit down, sit down, and I'll tell you. Some said old Mr. Gauthier made perfume out of his flowers, those last years of his life—you know, when he was retired. Poor old gentleman, he wasn't strong and Ma said he seemed mighty lonesome at the chateau. His son and daughter-in-law didn't pay much attention to him. Meant well, but— I don't know about that perfume tale. What I do know is his exquisite flowers."

When Pierre Gauthier's first flowers bloomed, from

seeds he had brought from France, neighbors flocked to the chateau to admire and marvel. None of them had seen the odd silver lace before, nor the rare fawn and China roses. His Provence roses, too, though akin to the American cabbage rose, were handsomer. The best roses in the world come from Provence. Molly Miller's mother had first seen his garden when she was a young girl, and recalled how generous Pierre Gauthier had been with his cuttings. No neighbor went away without prized flowers and shoots to transplant in his own garden. The silver lace was the most prized of all, for its delicate, delicious fragrance.

" 'Course," said Molly Miller, "it's one thing to grow flowers in any old fashion, and another thing to grow 'em right. You can't just transplant French flowers into American soil and climate. What Mr. Gauthier did as long as he was alive—and what Ma and me always did—was nourish those French flowers with extra care. Don't know as any other folks ever bothered. Neglect stunts 'em. We used extra-rich soil, a little more moisture, wrapped the bushes with burlap against cold, and I found a soil chemical that makes 'em— Well, I can rightfully say that my silver lace and French roses are equal to the ones the old gentleman grew." She proudly paused for breath.

Cherry was so excited she stuttered. Alan laughed and she started over.

"Mrs. Miller, have you silver lace and the French roses *now*? Can I purchase some, now, today, please?"

"Easy as pie," said Molly Miller. "How many would you like? Just a few of each, or two, three, four dozen?"

When Cherry arrived back at the school that afternoon with her arms full of the beautiful flowers, all the girls ohed and ahed and wanted to follow her and Alan into the infirmary.

Lisette came running. "So that's what Great-grandfather's flowers should look like and smell like when they're in a healthy state!" she said. "Mm, gorgeous! Oh, Cherry, Dr. Alan, I don't know how to thank you enough."

"Think nothing of it," said Alan. "Our nurse has informed me that I'm elected to help you two young ladies compound the perfume. It'll have to be in the evenings, but otherwise I'm your man. When do we start?"

Cherry and Lisette started immediately, for the freshly cut flowers could not wait. They did not need to detain the busy young doctor for the distillation of the natural flower oils. This second try went faster and easier than the first one. By eight that evening the girls had a precious sealed bottle of essential oils in the infirmary's refrigerator. As they washed and put away the kettle, saucepans, and tubing, Cherry and Lisette congratulated each other. This time the scent of the natural oils was the flowers' true scent.

Toward dusk the next afternoon, Alan arrived. He brought with him certain synthetics used by perfumers, notably, a rosy-smelling phenyl ethyl alcohol, which was an improvement and a short cut on the substances the great-grandfather had used. Mr. Clary had sent these. Mostly Alan brought with him a knowledge of chemistry which, added to Cherry's, should bring them closer to success. Lisette was relied upon to supply Pierre's notes and imagination as they began, that raw autumn afternoon, to recapture in scent the loveliness of a summer garden.

Step by step, they cautiously felt their way. Their base for the perfume was Pierre's flowers. Each time they added a drop of chemical to a drop of the natural flower oil, they tried the result on a clean blotter and sniffed. "Too sharp," Lisette would say, or Cherry's verdict, "Not clear cut." Alan would walk around the room, every few moments, sniffing the blotter again. "I don't like it." Another drop of synthetic bergamot, with its orangey-lemony fragrance of tart sweetness. Two drops more of ninety per cent alcohol. "No, the silver lace is drowned out now." They were trying hard to follow Pierre's notes exactly, but a hard-and-fast formula never yet created a distinctive perfume. They must rely on their own senses and judgment as well. A perfumer has to be both scientist and artist.

"Add a little ilang-ilang. Yes, that's better. I think we're beginning to put an odor together. Pierre's formula calls for a touch of vanillin, don't forget."

The three young people were fascinated by the drop-by-drop transformation. It was like an artist adding a touch of blue to his purple, then a dot of yellow, studying the mixture, and touching it ever so slightly with pink, to reach the shade he is seeking. They noted down each exact addition.

"It's shaping up, but it still doesn't blend."

"That's right, the Provence rose dominates too much. What does the textbook advise?"

"That silver lace makes your heart skip a beat, doesn't it? I thought only music could stir me that much," Alan admitted.

Absorbed, they forgot about suppertime. Mrs. Harrison sent up a tray of sandwiches and milk, and presently came in herself to visit.

"Oh! Rapturous!" She took a deep breath of the fragrant air. "Is your finished perfume going to smell like this?"

"That's the question none of us can answer, Aunt Alicia," said Lisette. "Will you be awfully disappointed if—well—"

"Dear Lisette, I've never ceased to be skeptical. But I most certainly am interested! You're fortunate in having two laboratory-trained friends to work with you."

"I don't know when I've had so much fun," Cherry said, and meant it.

Alan merely looked embarrassed and made a suggestion. Acting on it, they added to the by-now intricate compound a good deal more of the natural flower oil.

What happened was encouraging. Something had been lacking in the perfume, the three of them had felt all along. The perfume did not "ring true." Now the additional quantity of *natural* oils provided the missing link. The perfume grew at once more distinctive and more delicate. The note of silver lace was like a silver bell against the background of blended roses.

"I'm afraid to say it—" Cherry started.

"I think we have it!" Lisette muttered. "Don't you, Aunt Alicia?"

"I like *this,*" said Alan. "Agreed? Well, then." He pulled a small package out of his pocket. "I took the liberty of—ah—buying a better fixative than you girls may have used last time."

The fixative, besides retarding evaporation, also had to blend and harmonize the other ingredients. Cherry and Lisette were delighted with Alan's gift. Mrs. Harrison's sympathies had been growing as she watched.

"Did you know that when Catherine de Medici came from Italy to France to marry Henry II, she brought her own perfumer with her? His name was René, I think. This queen urged the cultivation of French flowers for perfume, and it's thanks to her that the French perfume industry came into existence."

Cherry, Lisette, and Alan were not really listening. They were trying to screw up courage to take the final, and possibly fatal, step—to add the fixative. Cherry realized suddenly that she was tired. It must be late.

Just then someone rapped at the door and Dr. Horton Wilcox came in.

"Good evening, Alicia, young ladies, Alan. I came over to talk with you, Alicia, about a fund-raising benefit we are planning for the hospital." The elder doctor's nose wrinkled and twitched. "All the balms of Paradise, eh?"

Mrs. Harrison invited Dr. Wilcox to sit down and asked if he would like some coffee.

"No, thank you, Alicia, very kind. What *is* going on here? This room smells like it used to when old Grandpa Gauthier occupied it."

Mrs. Harrison smiled. "Does it really smell the same? I've been trying to remember, but you always were observant and scientific-minded."

"Yes, very similar. I can still see old Pierre, in my mind's eye, puttering around this room, with vases and jars full of roses and *dentelle d'argent,* brewing his fragrances—"

"*Dentelle d'argent* translates into silver lace!" Lisette exclaimed. "We did get the name right. And we *are* on the right track, aren't we, Dr. Wilcox?" She named the flowers they were using. "You're an old settler, you'd know."

Dr. Wilcox laughed his restrained laugh. "Yes, I suppose I'm an old settler, old enough anyway to remember Pierre giving away flower cuttings. We children heard that he used his silver flower and his choicest roses for creating a perfume. Unfortunately, no one took him seriously. I've often thought—"

"*We* take him seriously," Lisette burst out. "I beg your pardon, I shouldn't have interrupted."

"Not at all, Lisette. I'm glad all of you do take his perfume seriously, because something quite fine may have been ignored or lost." The physician quoted Keats, " 'A thing of beauty is a joy forever. Its loveliness increases; it will never pass into nothingness.' "

"That settles it," Alan said. "With all this encouragement, let's go ahead and put in the fixative. Dad, do you want to wait for me or not?"

Mrs. Harrison laughed. "Your father can't tear himself away any more than I can. But I think we'd be wise to bow out."

They all exchanged good nights.

Alan brought out the fixative. With the utmost discretion a minute amount was added to the perfume-in-the-making. Cherry held her breath, for too strong a fixative could destroy the more delicate perfumes. Alan and Lisette seemed satisfied, though. Sniffing, they gradually increased the proportion of fixative until they obtained the desired balance.

"I'm not going to let you girls smell the result yet," Alan announced. He sealed the bottle and handed it to Lisette to store. "There'll be a coarse chemical smell for two or three days. The textbook says the flower freshness begins to—ah, Cherry, would you find and read that passage?"

"Yes, Doctor," Cherry said and read aloud, " 'At the end of a month the perfume will have lost its raw odor, a characteristic fragrance. All perfumes must go through an aging process.' "

"A month!" Lisette objected. "I'll expire of curiosity."

"Wait, there's more." Cherry read, " 'A peculiar

sweetness and flower freshness will develop after one week.' So we have to wait a week. Well, that's not as bad as a month."

Alan's only comment was that he was starving. Mrs. Harrison gave permission for Alan and the two girls to raid the kitchen. Finally the trio parted, sleepy but satisfied they had done their best.

Now it was purely a matter of waiting.

Lisette was so restless under the strain that she went through both of Pierre's notebooks again. The veiled passage in the journal about *la cloison,* the cubbyhole or enclosure, turned up again to puzzle her. It referred, as best she and Cherry could translate and interpret, to the staircase, the grand main staircase. Cherry suggested they ask Mrs. Harrison about it.

"*Cloison?* Near the staircase?" Mrs. Harrison thought for a moment. "Oh, you mean that little triangular storage space under the staircase where the stairs rise at a steep angle?"

"We don't know, Aunt Alicia. That area seems to be solid wood."

"No, it isn't, my dears. The people who founded the Jamestown School thought so, too, and never touched it, but I happen to know those panels are doors. It opens into a little space the family used as a catch-all, to keep rubbers and umbrellas. Odd, I had completely forgotten it. I had meant to clear it out. Why don't you look in there if you like? Though you'll probably find only some cobwebs. Give me until tomorrow to find the key."

Neither Cherry nor Lisette had seen a keyhole there. On looking, they found a tiny carved piece of wood at waist level. It resisted budging but finally it slid sideways, disclosing a keyhole beneath.

Next day the headmistress produced the key. Most of the girls had gone off to Riverton with their instructors for the day, to tour a museum, so Cherry and Lisette were able to explore without interruption.

On unlocking the triangular panels, a musty smell of wood and age floated out. Cherry felt around inside for an electric light; there was none, so she switched on her flashlight. She and Lisette stooped and stepped in. Dust, a heap of dried-up pairs of rubbers, a forgotten yellowed newspaper, were all they saw.

"Wait!" Cherry dug underneath the rubbers. "Here's a book. An old one. Must have been misplaced."

She blew the dust off it to see the title: *The Book of the Scented Garden*. They stepped out of the cubbyhole into the light and air of the entrance hall.

"What's the book's date?" Lisette asked. "It looks old enough for Great-grandfather to have used."

Cherry handed the book to Lisette, and in doing so, a blue envelope fell out and fluttered to the floor.

"A letter! What foreign-looking stationery. Cherry, just look at this postmark!"

The letter, addressed to Pierre Gauthier at the Chateau Larose, was postmarked Paris, France, in the same year he had died. Lisette's fingers shook so much, Cherry had to slip the letter out of the envelope for her.

Its letterhead was engraved with the name of one of the oldest and most famous of *parfumeurs.*

"Aunt Alicia! Aunt Alicia!"

"Mrs. Harrison, we found a letter!"

The three of them read it together, Lisette translating:

"My dear M. Gauthier: Our thanks for sending us the sample vial of your perfume creation. You will be pleased to know it reached us in excellent condition. Our head chemists and myself are much interested. You have achieved, it seems to us, a scent truly new and greatly appealing. Our house is actively interested in producing it. Naturally, there are problems of horticulture, chemical method, and costs which, as you yourself wrote to us, we need to discuss together. Would it be possible to meet with you in person? Of course at this first conference we do not expect anything beyond a general preliminary discussion. You can be sure we do not expect you to turn your detailed formula over to us unless and until we can reach an agreement on terms and royalties. We would suggest the month of June as a convenient and pleasant time. Assuring you of our admiration and interest, and with my kindest respects—"

Mrs. Harrison murmured, "Grandpa died in the month of June. He died on shipboard, on his way to Paris."

"Alone?" Cherry asked.

"Yes, alone. So near to seeing his dream fulfilled,

and then to die! Poor man! I never knew about this letter. None of the family knew. He never told us. We thought he took the trip for his health, and to visit some cousins."

"He never told you because you all teased him about his perfume making," Lisette chided gently. "How in the world, with practically all of his regular equipment plastered over, did Great-grandfather manage to make up a sample vial of perfume to send to France?"

"He must have made a superhuman effort." Mrs. Harrison shut her eyes for a moment, as if in pain. "Perhaps it's not too late for you two girls to right the wrong—a quite unintentional wrong—that was done to him."

"Well, the letter gives us reason to hope." Cherry brightened. "Why, this letter is powerful proof that Pierre's formula is valuable."

But whether they had recaptured his secret from the notes scattered in his two journals, or whether his secret had died with him, only the bottle waiting on the shelf upstairs would be able to reveal.

CHAPTER XIII

# *A Rare Perfume*

THE TELEPHONE RANG A FEW MINUTES BEFORE CHERRY was to meet Alan.

"Miss Cherry Ames, please." The voice sounded so dignified and far away that Cherry replied, "This is Miss Ames," and then realized she was being formal with her own mother.

"Cherry dear, do you think Charlie would enjoy turkey at home, or shall we go to Grandma's this year?"

"Wha-a-at?" Her mother, and her brother Charlie, too, spoke a family shorthand which was intelligible only if Cherry were at home to hear the earlier part of the conversation. "Please start at the beginning, Mother."

"Thanksgiving. It's next week. Don't tell me you've forgotten! You'll be home for Thanksgiving, won't you?"

"Well, I suppose so. If Mrs. Harrison—"

"I'll write to Alicia," Cherry's mother said, disposing of *that*. "Besides, Dr. Joe wants to talk with you."

"What about? Please don't keep me in suspense."

Her mother in Hilton laughed. "Dr. Joe is being mysterious, but I told him you'd surely come home for Thanksgiving."

"Of course I will, Mother. How are you and Dad?"

They talked a little longer, then Cherry hung up. As the telephone clicked, she heard Alan's car stop in the driveway.

Leaping Lena had been washed and polished for the occasion, and Alan's handsome face shone, too. It may have been due to the nippy air, or to pleasure in his companion. Cherry settled down in the front seat and opened the window wide.

"Where to?"

"Let's just ride," Cherry said. "And talk. How fast can this car go?" she asked to please him.

"Sixty easy. Seventy if I urge her. When Lena was younger, I got her up to ninety. Want to try it? This road's empty."

"No, thanks! I'm no speed demon. But Leaping Lena is a good girl."

"So are you. One of the best. Why don't we see each other oftener? Work, work, work!"

Cherry smiled and again said, "Let's just ride."

She and Alan were good enough friends by now to enjoy a comfortable silence together. They liked the same things—the sight of a red barn against the bright blue sky, the wind whipping in their faces, seeing a deer suddenly dart across the road and vanish among trees.

Cherry was grateful to him for taking her away from the chateau for a few hours. The tension of waiting out the balance of the seven days, while the perfume ripened, was difficult to put out of her mind. The perfume's outcome weighed on Alan, too. Both of them were making an effort to avoid talking about it, but when they stopped for a hot drink, the subject popped up.

"Have you and Lisette decided on a name for it? Or did old Pierre name it?"

"No, he didn't. I suppose the manufacturer will choose a name—that is, if it turns out well enough to interest your Mr. Clary or someone like him."

"Why not call it *Bride's Bouquet?*" Alan looked at her intently, across the booth table. "You know, Cherry, you're one of the prettiest girls I ever saw."

"Thank you."

"And one of the very best nurses I ever worked with."

"Oh, thank you! I hope you mean that, Alan."

"Sure I mean it. I mean it so much that I've been thinking—uh—maybe you and I could work more together. I mean, spend more time together—"

"Working?"

He was embarrassed but determined. His jaw stuck out. "Doctors and nurses make awfully good husband-

and-wife teams, too, you know." Then he just sat and looked at her and waited.

It was Cherry's turn to be flustered. "Why, Alan Wilcox! I never dreamed you liked me—er—seriously, I mean."

"Well, why do you think I monkeyed around making perfume? To please little Lisette? Or because I'm a great boy for perfume?"

They both burst out laughing.

"Oh, Alan, Alan, I've been dense." Cherry laughed at herself. "But I wish you hadn't dropped this bombshell on me. Do you realize how little we're really acquainted? How little time we've spent together?"

"We'll correct that," he said. "Now you tell me something. I have a suspicion that you're not going to spend the rest of your life in a school infirmary. Right?"

"Even if I should leave the school, I probably wouldn't be going very far. Only to my home town, Hilton, on the other side of the state. We'd see each other."

"For sure? Often? Is that a promise?"

"It's a promise."

Alan came to the school again on the eighth day. He could stay only a few minutes this time, he told Cherry, but it would not take long to learn whether their perfume had succeeded or failed. Lisette was trying to be very busy tidying up the now-repaired closet, on pins and needles until Mrs. Harrison came in. Then, without a word to one another they clustered at the shelf, before the all-important bottle.

"I can't stand the suspense," Mrs. Harrison gasped, laughing, and brushed back a strand of golden hair.

"And *you* were the doubter, Aunt Alicia!"

"Of course Alan's heart isn't really in this," Cherry teased.

"It is, too," he said gruffly. "What are we waiting for?"

"Now just a moment, my dears," said Mrs. Harrison. "I don't want any of you to be too terribly disappointed in case the experiment has not worked out. You did your very best, and that's the most anyone can do. When one follows a dream—"

"Here's where we wake up, one way or another." Alan reached for the bottle and, without further ceremony, broke the seal. "There's something powerful in here, good or bad. Lisette, you deserve to try it first."

Lisette carefully held the bottle in both hands, her dark head bent. She touched a drop to her wrist, inhaled, but only seemed puzzled. Mrs. Harrison extended her wrist for a drop; body warmth would bring out the full scent. They were all sniffing now.

"How funny," Lisette said shakily. "It doesn't smell anything like I thought it would. It doesn't even smell much like it did when we were making it."

"The textbook said that would happen," Cherry reminded her. "It's nothing to be discouraged about. The silver lace comes through delicate and true."

"Yes, it does," Mrs. Harrison said. "The blended roses form a kind of background for it."

"But the perfume is *raw,*" Lisette cried. "Crude!"

Alan had said nothing so far. "Of course it's raw, silly. It takes a month, at least, for perfume to ripen and we've allowed only a week. Try it again and try to imagine the essential scent without the rawness."

All four of them applied a bit to their wrists, and sniffed earnestly.

"Ah! It's emerging!" Mrs. Harrison exclaimed. "Mine has been warmed through by now and—well—it's magical! Oh, Lisette, this is an exquisite odor!"

"Or it's going to be when it's ripe," Cherry amended. "We have to remember our method of making it is awfully amateurish. A real perfumer would refine it and bring it to perfection. Mmm!"

She took a deep breath of the scent, and it seemed that the rarest flowers of France bloomed together in harmony. Something odd and poignant vibrated in Pierre's perfume. Probably it was the silver lace, the key to the perfume; somehow it touched the emotions as well as delighted one's senses.

Lisette was still afraid to believe what was becoming more and more unmistakable.

"It *is* rather unusual and—nice," she said.

The other three simply laughed at her. The most exciting thing was that the bottle held a genuinely different, distinctive perfume. Cherry ran through in her memory the various perfumes which she, her mother, and her friends had used, all lovely. But none like this!

"We ought to call it *Silver Lace,*" Lisette's voice broke in her joy. "Or *Fleurs de France.*"

"Or *Secret Rose,*" said Alan. "It certainly was a secret!"

" 'What's in a name?' " Alicia Harrison quoted. " 'That which we call a rose, by any other name would smell as sweet.' Ah, Lisette, how happy Grandpa would have been, if he could see us at this moment!"

"Perhaps he does know in some way," Lisette said gravely. "Or am I dreaming again?"

Alan pointed out that a brand-new perfume was no dream but a valuable property. What this bottle held was important enough to change their lives. Mr. Clary would surely be interested. There was a chance that the French perfume manufacturer, to whom Pierre had originally offered his creation, might renew his interest. More likely, some business arrangement would be worked out with Mr. Clary, who had contributed advice, raw materials, and encouragement, and then possibly also with the Parisian house. Lisette mentioned an outright sale of the formula, while Alan thought leasing the formula on a royalty basis to a manufacturer might be more profitable in the long run. In any case, Pierre's perfume was going to earn money for the Gauthiers and be a great help to the school.

"Aunt Alicia, now you won't have to worry any more about the mortgage on the school, or the roof—"

"Wait, wait! The perfume is yours, Lisette, because you had the spirit to find and develop it. Its earnings will go to you and your mother."

"Yes, it will make Mother's life much easier, that's so. And I'll be able to go on to college, now. I can even give you back my scholarship, to use for some other girl."

Mrs. Harrison said, "Well, we'll see."

Cherry had to smile at Lisette's independence and pluck.

"I'm going to attend the Jamestown School for the full four years, because I love this school for its own sake. And I think," Lisette rushed on, "that Cherry and Alan deserve a share, too."

Alan shook his head. "All I want is for you to name it *Bride's Bouquet.*" He stole a glance at Cherry. She wouldn't look back at him, saying to Lisette:

"Just send me a big, beautiful bottle of it for Christmas, some year."

They were so elated they chattered like a flock of birds. Cherry made an observation with which they all wholeheartedly agreed.

"Perhaps the best part of rescuing the perfume is that Pierre's devoted labor hasn't been wasted, and a lovely thing has been saved for many people to enjoy."

After the others had left the infirmary, Cherry noticed Mrs. Harrison had left her purse there. She took it downstairs to her. As she came into the office-study, she saw the antique doll propped up on the headmistress's desk. Mrs. Harrison sat smiling at the wooden manikin in its plum silk dress.

"Oh, thank you, Cherry, for my handbag. Do you know how old this doll is? She was 'born' in 1875, in France. She's only ten years younger than Pierre would be if he were still alive. I knew her when I was a little girl, and I haven't seen her until you found her again. You can imagine what it means to me to have her again."

"She guarded Pierre Gauthier's secret well, didn't she?"

"Indeed she did. Wedged in that bottom drawer—I never suspected! I'm glad that the previous tenants overlooked the old fruit-wood chest. It's stood down in the cellar since Pierre died, along with some other old furniture, and was so dilapidated that I didn't want it upstairs, either. That is, not until I ordered extra linens, about the time you came here this fall. Then it seemed to me extra drawer space in the infirmary might be handy, and I remembered the old chest."

Mrs. Harrison explained that she had sent Perry down to the cellar to dust off and polish the chest, and clear out its drawers, before bringing it upstairs to stand in the infirmary.

"Apparently Perry wasn't too thorough about going through the drawers," Mrs. Harrison said. "Or at least about the balky bottom drawer."

"I'm glad he wasn't, Mrs. Harrison. He might have

thrown away the bundle of rags, and the doll inside!"

They smiled at each other. The headmistress said: "Can you guess where our Lisette is? In the conservatory! I daresay she's imagining another perfume."

Cherry went on to the conservatory. Lisette had donned her blue smock and was cleaning out one of the beds.

"I'm so excited, I have to do something or I'll explode," she told Cherry. "I've put in a long-distance telephone call to my mother and I'm waiting for it to go through, so I can tell her our wonderful news."

"I'm so happy for you, Lisette."

Lisette looked up at her with her heart in her jet-black eyes. "If it hadn't been for your help, Cherry, there might not be any new, rare perfume. You're going to have a share in it."

"Thank you, but no, I'm not."

"Yes, you are."

"No, I'm not."

"Yes, you are." Lisette smiled broadly. "Anyway, we'll always be friends, won't we?"

"Of that I'm sure!"

A group of girls came surging into the conservatory. "Give me a rose, Lisette?" "What smells so wonderful? Who's wearing perfume?" "Will you *look* at the grin on Lisette's face! And Cherry's, too!"

They told the girls their marvelous news. All were delighted. Nancy and shy Mary, even Cora and Susan, hugged Lisette and offered their best congratulations.

If ever Lisette had been regarded as eccentric, that day was gone forever.

"We'll replant the conservatory," Lisette said eagerly. "You kids can help if you want to. There'll be roses enough for all of us. And in the spring, we'll make the garden bloom as it hasn't bloomed for years—"

Cherry smiled and left them to their plans.

She went back upstairs to her post, feeling happy all the way through. Her months as nurse at the Jamestown School could not have been more satisfying nor turned out more fortunately. She straightened her cap and gazed around the big, pleasant room, seeing in her mind's eye Nancy, Sibyl, Lisette, and a whole parade of girls whose health she had guarded. She looked with particular affection at the nursing utensils which had served them well in perfume making, then the closet which now breathed of old Pierre's presence. No matter how long or short a time she remained here as school nurse, she would go on to her next nursing adventure carrying a trail of perfume and happy memories.

The telephone rang. It was Alan.

"I forgot my penknife." Cherry glanced around the infirmary. He had done no such thing. Alan never forgot anything. "I'll drive right back to get it. Incidentally, can you come out to dinner with me?"

"Just give me time to change my dress and put on a little silver lace perfume," said Cherry. This, too, was a reward.